The Cloak of Dreams

ODDLY MODERN FAIRY TALES

Jack Zipes, *Series Editor*

Kurt Schwitters | *Lucky Hans and Other Merz Faiy Tales*

Béla Balázs | *The Cloak of Dreams: Chinese Fairy Tales*

The Cloak of Dreams
CHINESE FAIRY TALES

Béla Balázs

Translated and
Introduced by
Jack Zipes

Illustrated by
Mariette Lydis

PRINCETON UNIVERSITY PRESS   *Princeton and Oxford*

A portion of this book was first published in German
under the title *Der Mantel der Träume* by Bischoff in 1922.

Illustrations are reproduced from Béla Balázs, *Il libro delle meraviglie*, edited and
translated by Marinella D'Alessandro. Rome: Edizione e/o, 1994.

Published by Princeton University Press, 41 William Street, Princeton,
New Jersey 08540

In the United Kingdom: Princeton University Press, 6 Oxford Street,
Woodstock, Oxfordshire OX20 1TW

press.princeton.edu

Library of Congress Cataloging-in-Publication Data
Balázs, Béla, 1884–1949.
    [Mantel der Träume. English.]
    The cloak of dreams : Chinese fairy tales / Béla Balázs, translated and intro-
duced by Jack Zipes, illustrated by Mariette Lydis.
        p.   cm.   (Oddly modern fairy tales)
    "A portion of this book was first published in German under the title Der
Mantel der Träume by Bischoff in 1922."
    Includes bibliographical references.
    ISBN 978-0-691-14711-6 (hardcover : alk. paper)
    1. Tales—China.   2. Fairy tales—China.   I. Zipes, Jack, 1937–   II. Title.
GR335.B355 2010
398.20951—dc22

                                                            2009047839

British Library Cataloging-in-Publication Data is available

This book has been composed in Adobe Jenson with Myriad and Elli display.

Printed on acid-free paper. ∞

Printed in the United States of America

10 9 8 7 6 5 4 3 2 1

For Carol,
who's taught me that the
inspired man is the discerning man

■ Contents

Acknowledgments   *ix*

Béla Balázs, the Homeless Wanderer, or, The Man Who
Sought to Become One with the World   *1*

A Note on the Mysterious Illustrator Mariette Lydis   *58*

THE CLOAK OF DREAMS

1   The Cloak of Dreams   *65*
   Der Mantel der Träume

2   Li-Tai-Pe and the Thief   *70*
   Li-Tai-Pe und der Dieb

3   The Parasols   *74*
   Die Sonnenschirme

4   The Clumsy God   *80*
   Der ungeschickte Gott

5   The Opium Smokers   *86*
   Die Opiumraucher

6   The Flea   *90*
   Der Floh

7 The Old Child   *95*
Das alte Kind

8 The Robbers of Divine Power   *104*
Die Gottesräuber

9 Li-Tai-Pe and Springtime   *109*
Li-Tai-Pe und der Frühling

10 The Ancestors   *114*
Die Ahnen

11 The Moon Fish   *119*
Der Mondfisch

12 The Friends   *123*
Die Freunde

13 The Revenge of the Chestnut Tree   *133*
Die Rache des Kastanienbaumes

14 Tearful Gaze   *139*
Tränenblick

15 The Clay Child   *145*
Das Lehmkind

16 The Victor   *150*
Der Sieger

Appendix A | A Beautiful Book *by Thomas Mann*   *155*

Appendix B | The Book of Wan Hu-Chen *by Béla Balázs*   *159*

Bibliography   *173*

■ Acknowledgments

Special thanks to Barrie Tullett, who aroused my curiosity and led me to explore Balázs's fairy tales. As usual, Hanne Winarsky's enthusiasm and support has been the driving force behind this book. Once again, I am greatly indebted to Sara Lerner for carefully overseeing the entire production of *The Cloak of Dreams* and to Kim Hastings for her meticulous copyediting and helpful suggestions. Finally, I learned a good deal about patience and Taoism from Carol Dines, my wife, to whom this book is dedicated.

The Cloak of Dreams

■ Béla Balázs, the Homeless Wanderer, or, The Man Who Sought to Become One with the World

Everything is the symbol and fate of the soul. Everything
is the same stuff: *feeling and landscape, the thought and
the events of life, dream, and reality that are happening
around me. Everything is* one *stuff because everything is in
the same kind of way the fate of the soul and its revelation,
and it* exists!!! .... That's why I write fairy tales. *Now I
can explain it. Through its form the fairy tale symbolizes
that the glass mountain at the end of the world doesn't bring
dualism into my world. The fairy tale is also here on this
side. This feeling of unity could also be the conscience of the
new culture.*
—Béla Balázs, Letter to Georg Lukács (May 1910)[1]

Recognized internationally as one of the foremost film
critics and filmmakers in the early days of cinema, and famous for writing the libretto for Béla Bartók's opera *Bluebeard's Castle* in 1911, Béla Balázs was also a prolific writer
of fairy tales and a political activist who often compro-
mised his ideals to survive the turbulent years he spent in
exile, first in Austria and Germany during the 1920s and
then in the Soviet Union during the 1930s and 1940s. He
was not an easy man, but the times were not easy on him.
One of his biographers, Joseph Zsuffa, summarizes his
life as follows:

Béla Balázs was a complex character: a romantic and a utopian, a votary of materialism but also of mysticism, intrepid yet beset by cosmic fears, passionate yet gentle, most of all an eternal idealist. He lived in constant creative fervor, turning out cultural-philosophical essays, poems, short stories, art criticism, novels, plays, librettos, socio-political commentary, film scripts, and fables for adults and children. At times he was so tired that he cried from exhaustion. Balázs traveled a great deal, first for the pleasure of seeing the world and quenching his thirst for knowledge, later out of necessity, forced to live the life of an exile, and—toward the end of his life—driven by a desire to share his cinematic vision, in East and West, with filmmakers and film viewers alike.[2]

What Zsuffa fails to recognize is that Balázs was obsessed by fairy tales throughout his life, and that his life assumed the contours of the typical fairy-tale hero, the troubled young man who goes out to seek his fortune in the world. In Balázs's case, however, he desperately wanted to become one with an ideal world to which he could belong with heart and soul. Though he fought valiantly for his goal, he continually suffered bitter setbacks and often behaved callously. Balázs was still struggling and longing for utopian fulfillment when he died. If he found some hope and contentment, it was only as a writer and through his art. Along his arduous and solitary journey, he managed to produce unusual, mystifying fairy tales that did not mince words about the cruelty in the world, the twists of fate, and the courage and integrity that people needed to confront and transcend unjust conditions in turbulent Europe.

■

It is true that I proclaimed the synthesis of the nations, the European man. . . . It is true that I always felt my deepest metaphysical roots to be beyond every race and nation and I knew myself to be a wanderer, solitary. . . . It is true that according to my biological lineage, I am a Jew; thus, there is no more Turanian blood in me than there was in Sándor Petöfi. . . . And yet, what hurts? Why do I feel myself to be an exile?
—*Béla Balázs*, Diary (1920)[3]

Béla Balázs (pseudonym for Herbert Bauer) was born into a secular Hungarian-Jewish family on August 4, 1884, in Szeged, the second most important cultural city in Hungary. His parents, Simon Bauer and Jenny Levy, were teachers, and German was spoken at home, in part because Jenny Levy was from a German-Jewish family in East Prussia, but also because German was their "culture," so to speak. Balázs's father translated Goethe and Schiller, and both parents felt they were part of the German cultural tradition. Simon Bauer had studied in Vienna and Berlin before receiving his Ph.D. from the University of

Budapest. His first teaching position was at an advanced high school in Szeged, where he was active in liberal circles, regarded as a conscientious and dedicated teacher, and had plans eventually to become a professor in Budapest. However, in 1890, Bauer criticized and offended a Cistercian priest, his superior at his school, during an examination in which the priest had treated a poor student unfairly. Bauer refused to repent his courageous behavior, and as punishment, he was banished to Levoèa, a provincial town in the far north of the country, where he was cut off from intellectual stimulation and had virtually no contact with a Jewish community or important intellectual circles.

By this time Balázs had a sister, Hilda, born in 1885, and a brother, Ervin, born in 1890, and he attended a German Lutheran elementary school. Whereas his parents detested Levoèa and felt that they had been sentenced to a life in prison, Balázs was thrilled by the change in landscape and developed a love for the mountains that reminded him of fabulous scenes from fairy tales and picture books. He often took trips into the countryside to explore the mysterious world around him and felt at one with nature. However, this feeling of unity was rarely maintained, and if anything, Balázs felt more and more isolated if not ostracized from his Hungarian compatriots. Neither of his parents was religious, yet his father brought him secretly once a year to a minion on Yom Kippur to participate in a service that was anathema to Balázs. He was not permitted to participate in religion class at school because he was Jewish; during these lessons he was sent home, where he learned little more about Jewish culture or religion. In fact, Balázs's early years were marked by feelings of loneliness, marginalization, and trauma. Just as conditions appeared to be improving for his family in 1897, his father died suddenly from stomach cancer. That very same year, his mother, who had not worked in Levoèa, relocated the family to Szeged, where she began teaching once again, while Balázs attended the high school.

Although he felt at ease in Szeged and took frequent trips into the countryside to become better acquainted with peasant life, Balázs did not have many friends and spent hours at home, where he voraciously read the classics and important contemporary writers in German, French, and Hungarian. During his adolescence he had an unrequited love for Eszter Löw, the beautiful daughter of the city's leading rabbi, and she encouraged him to read Rilke's poems and J. P. Jacobsen's neoromantic novel *Niels Lyhne*. By the time he turned sixteen, he had begun writing a diary that he was to maintain on and off until his death. He had also decided that he wanted to become a writer and published some of his poetry in a local newspaper for the first time under the pseudonym Béla Balázs. The poems were written in Hungarian—a language he was urged to learn, but not the way Jews supposedly mangled it—and since the name Herbert Bauer seemed too German if not too Jewish, the young man was encouraged to adopt a pen name and kept using both Bauer and Balázs until he died.

He was called Herbert Bauer only by intimate friends. His ambivalence toward his given name and heritage reflected the dilemma that he shared with numerous middle-class Jewish intellectuals at the beginning of the twentieth century. As Hanno Loewy has remarked,

> Balázs's writing begins with the crisis that intellectuals experienced at the threshold of the twentieth century. The suffering from alienation motivated Balázs's tireless quest for a means of expression, a quest whose craze for experimentation reveled in romantic antirationalism and at the same time tested itself in various medias, genres, and types. . . . The restlessness of this quest revealed a deeply seated insecurity about the relations between human beings (felt as the social reification of domination) and between human beings and God (profanation), between human beings and their bodies (objectification), between human beings and things (dis-enchantment), and finally also about the alienation between the artist and the masses (the aestheticism that was suspected everywhere as being l'art pour l'art). This insecurity received its full and specific coloring by an entire generation of Jewish intellectuals from the assimilated bourgeoisie, who were stranded in Hungary at the turn of the century (and not only in Hungary) half way between emancipation and anti-Semitism, growing more and more radical, in a kind of social no man's land. These intellectuals endeavored

to resolve all this through conversion and cultural and political engagement in the society and found themselves simultaneously excluded by society.[4]

Confused about his identity but sensing that change was in the wind, the young Balázs worked assiduously to become a true Hungarian and felt a deep yearning to be at one with the Hungarian people. Clearly a gifted writer, he intended to demonstrate where he belonged through his art. With this goal in mind, he enrolled at the University of Budapest in 1902 after winning a scholarship.

Balázs's arrival in Budapest coincided with a great cultural renaissance. Hungary's fate had been tied to the Austro-Hungarian empire, that is, to Austria and Germany. But as the rising Hungarian middle class became stronger, more prosperous, and better educated, various groups formed heterogeneous political movements for independence and cultural rebirth. Along with a call for "authentic" and original Hungarian plays, operas, novels, music, and paintings, there was also a call for more "modern" works, and Balázs was more than ready to respond to both. Coincidentally, his roommate at the Eötvös Collegium, an institute of advanced studies established to develop exceptional teachers, was Zoltán Kodály, who would become one of the greatest Hungarian composers of the twentieth century and write the music for some of Balázs's poems and his opera librettos. At this point in his life, Balázs experimented in all forms of writing, and in 1904 he and Kodály joined the Thalia Society, founded by Georg Lukács, who was to become one of the eminent communist philosophers and literary critics in Europe. Lukács, as well as Kodály, had a profound influence on Balázs, and their endeavors in the Thalia Society led to the production of modern plays by writers such as Gerhard Hauptmann, Henrik Ibsen, August Strindberg, Frank Wedekind, and Maxim Gorky. Spurred by the society's modernist program, Balázs wrote unusual plays for the stage while studying German philosophy and the dramas of Friedrich Hebbel. By 1906 he formed another important friendship, with the experimental composer Béla Bartók, who would often travel into the countryside with Kodály and Balázs to collect folk songs and music from the peasants. Part of the "revolutionary" movement in the arts at that time involved a rediscovery of Hungarian folklore. The songs and tales that the three friends gathered played a strong role in Balázs's growing interest in fairy tales.

In the fall of 1906 Balázs won a stipend that would allow him to spend the next year studying in Berlin and Paris. In Berlin he participated in Georg Simmel's private seminar and wrote one of his most important essays, "The Aesthetics of Death," which was to determine a crucial aspect of Balázs's pantheistic outlook on life. For Balázs, death did not signify an end of life. Rather, it gave life its meaning. Balázs's focus in this sprawling essay filled with original postulates is on the relationship of art to death, and how art is the manifestation of the metaphysical instinct and enables the artist to endow his or her work with transcendental and religious significance. According to Balázs, "consciousness of life is only possible through death. . . . The prerequisite for the consciousness of life is death. That is, death is the prerequisite of art. Death endows life with shape. Its end is like the contour of a drawing, the limit of the figure, which gives it shape."[5] The paradox of death is that it generates a sensitivity toward life that allows us to feel the entirety of life, our mortality, and our eternity. Prompted by death, artists create various forms and genres to embrace life, give it significance, and delineate it from nonexistence. One form is the fairy tale, and Balázs discusses its paradoxical quality in relation to death: "The fairy tale does not yearn, does not look outside itself. It does not go in one direction and does not want to get to the root of anything. It remains introspective and plays kaleidoscopically with what's there. The fairy tale does not have any limits, and consequently, it is also not without limits. It does not want to understand anything, and consequently, there is nothing that it doesn't understand. Its wide sea also has its distant shore, and consequently, it is also not a lonely island. The fairy tale is without consciousness. The feeling of transcendence is a feeling of it-does-not-go-further-than-here, and this feeling is exactly what the fairy tale does not know. The common people do not claim the novel or novella; they only have anecdotes, fairy tales, and legends."

It is fascinating to see how Balázs, even before he began writing his major fairy tales, had already signaled his great interest in this genre by 1907 and attributed its origins to the common people. Also interesting is how he links fairy tales to instincts and pantheism. Notably, he dedicated the essay to Simmel when it was published in Hungarian in 1908. One of the foremost sociologists and philosophers of that time, Simmel stressed that knowing the world demanded intuitive thinking. Simmel's ideas enabled the fanatical romantic anticapitalist Balázs to formulate his mystical urges in metaphysical and poetical terms, and these urges were tied to the main concerns of his life—marginalization, lack of identity, the experience of alienation, or alienation as the basic condition of human beings. Ferenc Fehér has summarized precisely how important Simmel's philosophy was for Balázs:

> It was from this school that he created his central poetical experience: *the alienatedness of human existence*. . . . However, I am not using the term "experience of alienation" in a banal sense, as this category has been used ever since its fashionable philosophical clearance sale. The question does not simply concern how to describe each and every human misery and distortion of the late bourgeois society, of the *fin de siècle*, as a symptom of alienation. Balázs felt and sensed vaguely and with a great deal of yearning that there must be something humanly essential behind "the gates of life," something that the forces of life (also conceived vaguely) have ripped from us. For the artist

there is only one categorical imperative: to contribute to the reconquering of the essential world that has been ripped from us.[6]

When Balázs returned to Budapest in the fall of 1907 after a brief visit to Paris, he continued to be inspired by Simmel and other thinkers who wrote about the alienated condition of human beings and the lack of communication that fostered desolation and isolation. These ideas formed the substance of poems, stories, plays, and articles, many of which were at first not accepted for publication. It is not by chance, however, that Balázs's first success in fiction was a fairy tale, "Die Stille" (Silence), which appeared in *Nyugat* (Western), a new literary journal, which promoted modernist art and literature and became one of the most prominent periodicals in Hungary in the first half of the twentieth century.[7]

"Silence" is highly significant because it indicates in form and content how Balázs cultivated the fairy tale as genre to pursue his mystical notion of identity and to celebrate his oneness with the world in opposition to the forces of alienation. The plot of this tale is simple and recalls age-old folk motifs that lend the narrative a rustic, poetic quality. (It is worth mentioning that Hermann Hesse, Hugo von Hofmannsthal, and other European writers such as Knut Hamsun were embracing both Asian and European fairy tales and folklore at this time to pry at the essence of life.)

In Balázs's story, a naive young man by the name of Peter watches his sick mother in a hut in the mountains as she is about to die. She asks him to fetch some firewood outside, where the fairy Silence has been waiting and watching him for some time. She is in love with him and represents his destiny, but Peter is frightened by Silence literally and figuratively. So he runs inside, where he is given a magic ring by his dying mother, who explains how it will help him find his destiny: he must place the ring on the finger of the person whom he loves most and who is intended for him. If he chooses the wrong person, he or she will die, and the ring will return to his finger until he finds the right person. Grief-stricken, Peter immediately places the ring on his mother's finger, but she dies because she is the wrong person. All at once Silence appears and tells him to place the ring on her finger. He refuses and flees. Soon he joins a wandering musician named Paul, and they spend many happy months together until Paul decides to become an apprentice to the Father of the Grotto, who creates fantastic music in the mountains. Peter puts the ring on Paul's finger to try to keep him and maintain their friendship. However, Paul dies, and the fairy Silence reappears demanding the ring. Once again Peter flees but eventually falls in love with a factory worker named Ilona. The two share an intense relationship that falls apart when Ilona rejoices in silence. Indeed, she dies, and Silence again appears to claim the ring. Peter refuses to yield to the fairy and returns to the mountains, where he finally realizes that he must succumb to his fate and bestow the ring on Silence, who lives at the bottom of a lake on a snowy mountain. It is there that Peter loses and finds himself in mysterious depths.

All the fairy-tale motifs and themes that recur in Balázs's fairy tales, plays, poems, librettos, and stories can be found here—the wandering protagonist seeking the essence of life, mysterious woods and mountains, haunting music, pure friendship, passionate love, solitude, alienation, magical objects, and pantheistic ecstasy in a liminal state. Balázs turned the fairy tale into an enigma and harked back to the great German romantic fairy tales of W. H. Wackenroder, Ludwig Tieck, Novalis, and E.T.A. Hoffmann. Like these German writers who imbued the *Kunstmärchen* (the literary fairy tale) with complex philosophical notions that distinguished it from the oral folktale, Balázs believed that there was a primeval spirit in the fairy tale that had to be cultivated to enable him and his readers to transcend their existential dilemma. To recapture this spirit, Balázs gave the language and plot of the fairy tale a mysterious quality that he sought to elaborate in various forms and with diverse media throughout his life. In this regard, he had a paradoxical relationship to modernism: he sought to recuperate and retain the traditional forms of storytelling while radically changing the contents and plots. Balázs's fairy tales dismiss material happiness and traditional marriages in favor of ecstasy and transcendence. One cannot overcome feelings of loneliness and alienation in a relationship or marriage, but through forms of art that merge with the cosmos.

Following the publication of "Silence," Balázs was able to publish "The Aesthetics of Death" and some other short pieces in different magazines and journals that promoted the work of young, experimental writers. At the same time, he concentrated on finishing his studies for employment purposes. (Balázs was poor and often borrowed money from his rich friends, especially Lukács.) In September of 1908 he received his doctorate by writing and defending a dissertation on the German dramatist Friedrich Hebbel. After serving a month in the Hungarian army, he began teaching at a high school in Budapest to support himself while he wrote plays for the theater. Though Lukács championed Balázs as one of the most formidable young playwrights in Hungary, Balázs's plays had only a limited success during this period.

From 1909 to 1911 his artistic production was prolific, and his friendship with Lukács, who at this time was more influenced by German idealism and formalism than communism, deepened. They appeared to be destined for one another as spiritual friends in a kind of elective affinity.[8] Meanwhile, Balázs, who had numerous affairs, began a relationship with Edith Hajós, a student of medicine at the University of Budapest. She was the daughter of a wealthy lawyer who had converted from Judaism to Catholicism. A brilliant but apparently unstable woman, Edith was to play a major role in Balázs's life. They married in 1913 after Balázs converted to Catholicism to please her and her family and gain their trust. However, marital fidelity was a phrase that never entered Balázs's vocabulary. He rarely controlled or wanted to control his libido, and while he was engaged to Edith, he had a brief relationship with Irma Seidler, a gifted painter who happened to be Lukács's partner. Meanwhile, Lukács was interested in having an affair with Balázs's sister, Hilda. In the circles in which Balázs and Lukács moved, free love was part of the revolutionary movement, but there were always casualties. When Irma Seidler, who had always been troubled, committed suicide in 1911 for unknown reasons, Balázs hesitated for a long time to tell Lukács about his affair, causing a temporary breach in their friendship. In 1914 Balázs encountered another woman, Anna Schlamadinger, who was married to a wealthy judge. Within a year, she left her husband and formed a threesome with Balázs and Edith, who had come to accept her as a second wife. Eventually, Edith separated from them, and Balázs married Anna, who remained with him until his death. And until his death, Balázs continued to have affairs and would find solace in the forgiving arms of Anna.

Balázs's "entanglements" with women will never be wholly unraveled, but they are important to consider when interpreting his artistic works: love as rapture and ecstasy and the representation of women associated with orgiastic death are constant motifs. Never, however, are the relationships with women based on mutual understanding. A good example is his adaptation of Charles Perrault's fairy tale "Bluebeard." In 1909, when Balázs met Edith, he was working on a mystery play, which he eventually titled *A kékszakállú herceg vára* (*Bluebeard's Castle*). He finished the play in 1911 and dedicated it to Bartók and Kodály. After he published it in a theater magazine, he offered it to them as a libretto for an opera. Since Kodály did not find it suitable for his work, Bartók took on the project and began composing the score in 1911. He made some revisions in 1912, but the onset of World War I meant that the opera was not performed until 1918. Because of the radically mystical libretto and the complex musical score, the work was not particularly well received.

Indeed, in Balázs's modernist reinterpretation of the serial killer Bluebeard, the protagonist is transformed into some kind of intrepid mysterious lover, whose power over the women he has loved is eternal and unquestionable. The one-act opera begins in a dark hall in a castle. Bluebeard has just arrived with his new wife, Judith, with whom he has eloped. She perceives that there are seven locked doors in the hall and wants to open them to bring light into the gloomy interior. At first Bluebeard refuses to allow her to do this, declaring that the rooms are his private spaces, and if she loves him, she will not explore them. However, Judith insists that it is exactly because she loves him that she needs to know these secret places. Bluebeard relents, and one by one the doors are unlocked. The first reveals a torture chamber, stained with blood; the second, a room filled with weapons; the third, a treasure chamber of gold and jewels; the fourth, a beautiful garden; the fifth, a huge window that opens onto Bluebeard's splendid estate. Once the huge hall is fully lit, Bluebeard tries to convince Judith to stop. But she refuses and opens the sixth door, which reveals a glistening silver lake of tears. Bluebeard pleads with her not to ask any more questions and to trust his love for her. But Judith is curious and wants to know about his former wives and whether he has murdered them. She insists that the bloodstained rooms and the tears come from his wives and that their bodies lie behind the seventh door. At this point, Bluebeard hands her the seventh key, and when Judith unlocks the last chamber, three beautiful women emerge dressed in marvelous gowns with sparkling jewels. Bluebeard throws himself at their feet and praises them. Then he proceeds to laud Judith as his fourth wife and adorn her with heavy jewels. She is horrified, but he continues, and once he is finished, she follows the other three wives back into the seventh room lit by moonlight. When the door closes, Bluebeard stands alone and is enveloped by the darkness.

This mystery play is a very bizarre redemption of Bluebeard, that is, of men who sequester their wives as beautiful objects that decorate the internal chambers of their castle, perhaps symbolic of the heart and soul of men.[9] On an autobiographical level, the play can be read as Balázs's enduring vision and treatment of women, who were not to ask questions about a man's innermost feelings, behavior, and beliefs just as long as he adored them. They were to succumb to his taciturn power. On a philosophical level, the play can be understood as an exploration of the fathomless soul. The solitary Bluebeard's secrets seem to be unlocked, and yet they are never fully revealed. Bluebeard will live on in solitude and mystery. Questions are all that remain: Are the doors to the chambers of his life and soul representative of experiences that have led to dismal solitude? Can we ever know the identity of a person? Should love ever be questioned? *Bluebeard's Castle* does not provide clear answers to these questions, but it certainly reveals Balázs at his narcissistic best.

In comparing Lukács's view of aesthetics to Balázs's perspective, Ferenc Fehér makes the following astute observation: "In the process of analyzing the differences, we shall see that Balázs's aesthetics is just as much a theory of art of Narcissus as is his theory of the drama a poetics of Narcissus. . . . The first difference arises seemingly from a methodological approach, namely that Balázs writes an 'aesthetics of the artist,' while Lukács conceives a 'general' philosophy departing from aesthetics (or even remaining within it)."[10] Clearly, there is a strong element of narcissism in everything Balázs did or wrote, but more important, despite Balázs's socialist leanings, is that he depicted the solitary, ascetic hero and art as the means through which one is to overcome alienation, not political revolution, as Lukács did.

Balázs's play about Bluebeard was not the only drama or mystery that Balázs wrote during this time to explore his male fantasies. For instance, in 1912, he also published another mystery play, *A tündér* (The Fairy), in which a fairy causes a young couple to abandon their idyllic love for each other by inspiring them to pursue adventure and higher ambitions. The 1914 fairy tale "A három huséges királyleány" (The Three Faithful Princesses) depicted yet another intrepid hero, a powerful king named Suryakanta, who believes that deeds speak more than words and who is referred to as a tiger, fierce and stern. When he goes into the jungle one day to do penance, he comes across a black snake that he kills because his soul is arrogant and hard. All at once the elephant god Ganesha appears and punishes him by separating him from his hard soul. Suryakanta is transformed and becomes soft and servile. His loyal servant Rasakosha barely recognizes him, and his beautiful wife Balanpandita rejects him. Suryakanta himself feels that he has lost his stature and identity as king. So he returns to the jungle in search of his identity and a faithful woman who will anchor his soul. After wearing a mask of his former self, he believes he has found a soul mate in the princess Kamailila, but she fails him when put to a test. He becomes bestial and then resumes his kingly shape cleansing himself in a lotus pond. Finally, he is drawn to the princess Anangaraga, Kamailila's sister, and asks her what would happen if he were to change. "Suryakanta cannot change," she responds. "Among men Suryakanta is what the diamond is to all the stones: glistening, pure and hard. The flower of his life is rooted in previous lives and cannot move itself or change."[11] Upon hearing these words, Suryakanta realizes that Anangaraga is his soul mate and makes her his wife. Together they go back to his palace where the eternally loyal Rasakosha greets the returning king.

Though Balázs called Anna Schlamadinger his Anangaraga as a pet name, and though he demanded absolute loyalty from her and other women as well as his male friends, Balázs could never become the resolute sovereign he imagined himself to be, or wanted to be. The years that followed the publication of this fairy tale saw Balázs constantly changing his perspective on life and pursuing idealistic goals that led to his attachment to and "glorification" of communism.

When World War I erupted in June of 1914, he rejoiced and immediately sought to enlist in the Hungarian army. As Zsuffa remarks, "Balázs believed in 'individual conscience and individual responsibility.' He considered it his moral duty to break out of his isolation, to offer his life for the community. His mysticism gave way to a 'mystical anarchism.'"[12] Unlike many of his friends who opposed the war, such as Lukács, Balázs felt that war was sacred and would constitute some kind of cleansing act. However, when he was finally sent to the front in Serbia as a common soldier, he experienced the barbaric nature of war and the suffering caused by it, and he no longer glamorized it. After serving three months in Yugoslavia, he became critically ill and was sent home. When he had fully recuperated in the spring of 1915, he resumed his former life in Budapest, writing, teaching, maintaining his relationship with Edith and Anna, and having affairs. One relationship with a young woman named Eszter Grad turned tragic when she committed suicide. Though Balázs did not blame himself for her death, he was disturbed and began living alone. In the fall of 1915, to overcome his solitude, he began inviting friends to his apartment in Budapest on Sunday afternoons to discuss philosophy, the arts, and culture. Most of the members of the group called the Vasárnapi kör (Sunday Circle), including Lukács, Kodály, Bartók, Arnold Hauser, Friedrich Antal, Karl Mannheim, Wilhelm Szilasi, Charles de Tolnay, Anna Lesznai, René Spitz, and others, became leading intellectuals and writers of the twentieth century.[13] At that time they were not active in politics and were more interested in a cultural revolution than a political one. As part of their program, they founded the Free School of Humanistic Sciences, where Balázs occasionally held lectures. For the most part, however, he focused on his writing—mystery plays, the ballet *A fából faragott királyfi* (The Wooden Prince) for Bartók, a volume of poetry, as well as *Lélek a háborúban* (Soul in War), a journal about his experiences in World War I.

By 1917 Balázs had completely changed his views of the war, which he now opposed, and drew closer to Lukács. In fact, their friendship, which Lukács referred to as a brotherhood in arms, had reached its highest point, especially with Lukács's publication of an entire book dedicated to Balázs in early 1918, *Béla Balázs and Those Who Do Not Want Him*.[14] A brilliant critic, Lukács wrote sincerely about the significance of Balázs's early works, in particular his mystery plays:

> Surely, few poets live today whose artistic forms are so deeply rooted in the forms of human experience and grow so naturally out of them as is the case with Béla Balázs. That is why his development has been so slow and difficult: he is a naive poet in the most serious sense of the word; he expresses his own experiences alone, and does not have either the gift or the inclination to hide with skillful tricks anything that has not grown to perfection in him, that is still only incomplete in him. But precisely because his tremendous artistic talents are *a priori* linked to the eternal forms, because he approaches them not as historical circumstances, which can only be seen from the distance of historical perspective, but returns to them as to natural forms of expression for the innermost contents of his own soul, his path to reaching perfect solutions was very difficult. His "naturalistic tendencies" resisted the similarly vital aspiration for concise form, and he was able to achieve ripeness as an artist only when he was able to resolve this conflict.[15]

Indeed, Balázs had come into his own as a writer. In early 1918 *Hét mese* (Seven Fairy Tales), a collection of stories, some of which had appeared in *Nyugat* and included *The Wooden Prince*, was published, as well as *Kalandok és figurák* (Adventures and Figures), his sketches and novellas. Active as ever, he signed a contract to write a libretto for the Medgyaszay Theater in Budapest and joined a league of intellectuals with Lukács called the Knights of Europe to protest against militarism and nationalism. His wife Edith, who had traveled to Russia and spent several months there learning Russian, fell in love with a doctor, returned to Budapest, and asked for a divorce, which Balázs readily granted because he was more in love with Anna. The two separated amicably and maintained a close relationship throughout their lives.

By the fall of 1918 the Austro-Hungarian empire was collapsing, and Balázs joined the growing radical movement to establish an independent Hungary. Despite the fact that a republic was established in November, there was still great discontent among the populace, and the newly formed Hungarian Communist Party led by Béla Kun began fomenting unrest and demanded greater democratic reforms. Lukács became a member of the Communist Party, and though he supported his friend and his cause, Balázs withdrew from political activism because of ethical reservations. However, in March of 1919, as conditions in Hungary deteriorated, and the communists assumed control of the government and declared the country to be the Hungarian Soviet Republic, Balázs became politically active once again thanks to Lukács, who was appointed deputy commissar of public education. In this capacity, Lukács assigned Balázs a position on the Writers Directorate in charge of literary affairs in the new republic. Aside from developing theater policy, Balázs established a fairy-tale department and appointed his friend Anna Lesznai to be one of the officials who supervised puppet plays and storytelling for children in theaters and schools. Ever since his childhood, when he used to listen to tales told to him by his father and the peasants in the countryside, Balázs felt strongly that folk and fairy tales provided the joy in life connected to the essential experiences of the common people. Though he was criticized for promoting fairy tales by hard-line communists who claimed they were too unrealistic and furthered feudal and capitalist thinking, Balázs responded that storytelling formed the roots of all poetry and enabled children to grasp the deep meaning of community. It was through folklore, Balázs always hoped, that he might overcome the alienation he had felt since childhood, and it was through communion with the folk, he believed idealistically, that a new society could be created.

During the four-month existence of the Hungarian Soviet Republic, Balázs worked tirelessly to inject a utopian spirit into all the cultural projects he developed. While Lukács regarded communism from the viewpoint of a policy maker who at times ruthlessly ordered the destruction of all enemies, Balázs remained an idealist who came to believe in communism as a religion and a means through which he might find his true community. However, there was too little time to establish a strong socialist, not to mention communist, society in Hungary, and the Hungarian Soviet Republic was soon attacked by Romanian and Czechoslovakian forces in April of 1919 with the support of England, France, and America. In response, both Balázs and Lukács went to the battle front to join the Hungarian Red Army and fight for their different communist beliefs. Before he left Budapest, Balázs married Anna Schlamadinger, fearing that he might never see her again.

But Balázs was a survivor. When the Hungarian forces were finally defeated and the leading members of the Hungarian Soviet Republic surrendered and were granted diplomatic immunity on August 1, 1919, Balázs fled to Budapest and went into hiding. With the help of friends he managed to escape the police, and disguised as his brother, he eventually made his way to Vienna by traveling via boat on the Danube with Anna by his side. Although he did not know this at that time, Balázs was to spend the next twenty-five years in exile as a political refugee in Austria, Germany, and the Soviet Union, often living under dire circumstances.

■

Everything depends on our spiritualizing communism into
a religion. That is our mission. There are so many today
with hungry hearts; more than ever before.
—Béla Balázs, Letter to Anna Lesznai (1921)[16]

There were numerous friends (and enemies) in the Hungarian exile community of Vienna. Many of the members of the Sunday Circle, including Karl Mannheim, Polányi,

Lesznai, and Lukács, were there and lived in fear that they might be extradited. It was difficult for most of them to find employment, and since Balázs had been raised with German as his "mother" tongue, he now decided to write and publish mainly in German, intuiting that his Austrian exile might be of long duration. One of his plays, *Halálos fiatalság* (Deadly Youth), written in 1917, was translated and to be performed by the Neue Wiener Bühne in Vienna, and he spent a good deal of his time rewriting the German translation and directing the play. In the meantime, he and Anna had to move from boarding house to hotel to boarding house in search of an affordable dwelling. They finally rented a small house in Reichenau, outside Vienna, thanks to the financial help of his former wife, Edith, who had left Russia and suddenly appeared in Vienna. Meanwhile, Balázs met the famous Danish writer Karin Michaelis, with whom he began writing a novel, *Túl a testen: Egy férfi és nö naplója* (Beyond the Body: Diary of a Man and a Woman, 1920), and he managed to make a meager living by writing plays, pantomimes, poems, essays, screenplays, and stories. Some of his works, such as the novel *Isten tenyerén* (On God's Palm, 1921), were still being published in Hungary or in Hungarian exile magazines.

As his interests turned more and more toward writing screenplays and film criticism for German and Austrian newspapers, he received a strange offer. Genia Schwarzwald, a wealthy Austrian patron of the arts and founder of an exclusive private school for girls, had known Balázs before the Hungarian Revolution, and when he came to Vienna in 1919, she had provided financial assistance and also introduced him to Karin Michaelis. In September of 1921, she learned that her friend Mariette Lydis, a talented painter and illustrator, was looking for a writer who might create stories based on twenty aquarelles in Chinese figurative style that she had composed.[17] Schwarzwald contacted Balázs, who was then hired by Lydis after he submitted two tales that met with her approval. However, there was an urgent deadline, and Balázs was expected to write sixteen tales within three weeks. Intrigued by the challenge, Balázs, who had a great interest in Asian art, went to work immediately and punctually delivered the tales that were to form the book *Der Mantel der Träume: Chinesische Novellen* (*The Cloak of Dreams: Chinese Fairy Tales*, 1922), published in Vienna. Steeped in Taoist philosophy, these tales are among the best he ever wrote and reflected Balázs's profound personal concerns about friendship, alienation, poetry, transformation, and transcendence. Aside from a glowing review by Thomas Mann (see appendix A), the book received little attention, but Balázs thought so highly of it that he himself translated it into Hungarian in 1948 with a new title, *Csodálatosságok könyve* (*The Book of Marvels*), which represented his enduring faith in the metaphorical power of fairy tales to express his philosophical beliefs.

It is not by chance that in 1921, at a key point in his life, Balázs produced these fairy-tale gems in his mother tongue.

Indeed, he never stopped creating fairy tales in either German or Hungarian, even though he moved more and more toward writing screenplays and writing about film as the highest form of art. But film, to his mind, had to be commensurate with the fairy tale. In his incisive analysis of Balázs's life and poetics, Hanno Loewy comments:

Already in his earliest philosophical fragment about art, "The Aesthetics of Death," Balázs points to the fairy tale—beyond its significance as genre— also as a medium in which yearning and expression would blend into "truth of form," which is even more important than the "truth of content." Balázs's turn to film, for which he certainly never abandoned his interest in fairy tales, dramas, and prose, will be interpreted here as an endeavor to establish a popular medium within the context of the modern, technologized mass society commensurate with the fairy tale, a medium that would be capable of offsetting alienation in a ritual and controlled act of initiation into a state of unity between life and cultural form—at the cost, to be sure, of exchanging the true wish fulfillment for an act of visual union with the object of desire. His interpretation of film does not aim for the avant-garde, rather for a new folk culture and a new narrative tradition. The vanishing point of Balázs's aesthetics of the cinema is the imaginary enchantment of the world into a visual ritual of storytelling.[18]

From 1921 to 1926 Balázs developed his notions of film as art form in his reviews for the Berlin communist paper, *Die Rote Fahne*, and also for the liberal Viennese newspaper *Der Tag*, which provided him with his own column. He wrote well over two hundred articles for these publications, some of which became part of his first major book on film, *Der sichtbare Mensch oder die Kultur des Films* (The Visible Man or the Culture of Film, 1924). This work celebrated film as a new and revolutionary art form because it transcended print and breathed life into culture by giving humanity an actual face that could express the needs and wishes of people in a profound way. Balázs wrote not only about the cinema but also about the theater, cultural events, and art. This was also the period in which he began writing screenplays for Hans Otto Löwenstein, primarily to make money, but also as a kind of apprenticeship that would enable him to learn more about the production of films.[19] Aside from his work in the cinema, he was active in the newly founded Free School, which had been transplanted to Vienna from Budapest; participated in various cultural movements for peace, such as Clarté, founded by Henri Barbusse and Romain Rolland; and formed friendships with some of the leading German and Austrian writers living in Vienna, such as Robert Musil and Arthur Schnitzler. As a communist party sympathizer, he wrote short propaganda plays and prose pieces for the party's celebrations, donated money and time for communist causes, and continually placed himself at the service of the party's clandestine operations. In the meantime, he became the foremost cultural and film critic in Austria and was able to lead a more comfortable life with Anna, who worked as a secretary, in Vienna. A prolific writer, he never abandoned the fairy tale and published *Das richtige Himmelblau* (The True Skyblue), a collection of three fairy tales for young readers, in 1925. Interestingly, all three tales, "Brother Country," "The True Skyblue," and "The Brave Machine Boy, the Old Toad, and the Big Multiplication Table," are imbued with utopian notions of an alternative realm. The protagonists, all children, learn to cope with problems in the real world by experiencing otherness or entering into another condition. It is through otherness that unification is achieved or conflicts are resolved.

His conception of fairy tales as transformative media that could immerse the reader or listener in another human condition went hand in hand with his conception of screenplays and cinema as transformative art. Since the film industry in Austria, was in a crisis, however, Balázs realized that he had to seek opportunities elsewhere to pursue his career as critic and scenarist, namely, in Berlin. In June of 1926 he held a lecture at the Klub der Kameraleute (Cameramen's Club) in which he praised the cameraman as the lyricist of the film. Aside from fomenting a quarrel with Sergei Eisenstein, the pioneer Russian filmmaker, who criticized him for his "bourgeois" glorification of the cameraman as artist, Balázs was able to impress producers and filmmakers and make contacts that would enable him to support himself as a screenplay writer and critic in Berlin. After he received a commission from Karl Freund of Fox Europa Production to write the scenario for Berthold Viertel's *Die Abenteuer eines Zehnmarkscheins* (The Adventures of a Ten-Mark Note), he moved permanently to Berlin with Anna in the fall of 1926.

After an auspicious beginning and success with another film, Alexander Korda's *Madame wünscht keine Kinder* (Madam Wants No Children, 1926), Balázs had nothing but problems with the German film industry. He wrote the screenplay for *Doña Juana* directed by the Hungarian filmmaker Paul Czinner, but he was so unhappy with the final product that he demanded that his name be withdrawn from the credits. In a second project with Czinner, an adaptation of Arthur Schnitzler's play *Fräulein Elsie*, he had another argument and sued Czinner once more to have his name deleted from the credits. After these two incidents, Balázs was regarded as persona non grata in the film industry. However, in 1929 an independent filmmaker, Alfred Abel, hired him to write the scenario for *Narkose* (Anaesthesia), which was based on a novella by Stefan Zweig. Indeed, Balázs continued to find work as a scenarist outside the large studios.

As usual, he did more than write screenplays while he was in Berlin. Aside from giving lectures in Marxist clubs, writing hundreds of articles and reviews for different newspapers and important left-wing journals such as *Die Weltbühne*, serving on the executive board of the German

Film Authors' Association, promoting the union work of the Main Organization of German Film Creators, and supporting communist causes, Balázs worked with the famous Marxist director Erwin Piscator, with whom he endeavored to produce an agit-prop play, wrote the libretto for a ballet *Mammon* with music by Ernst Krenek and another libretto for Wilhelm Grosz's opera *Achtung Aufnahme* (Camera! Action!), produced in 1930. One of his more interesting collaborations was with Lisa Tetzner, a notable storyteller and writer of children's books, who published a remarkable fairy-tale novel, *Hans Urian geht nach Brod* (Hans Urian Goes in Search for Bread, 1929). This book, based on a poem by Matthias Claudius and a French novel, *Jean sans Pain* (Jean without Bread, 1921), by Paul-Vaillant Couturier, recounts the fabulous adventures of a poor young boy named Hans, who sets out to buy some bread for his starving mother. However, he encounters some difficulties and does not grasp why it is so difficult to buy bread. At one point, he meets a marvelous rabbit who can talk and fly and is willing to take him on a trip to explain how capitalism is based on exploitation and why people are suffering from hunger. They fly around the world, to Greenland, America, Africa, India, China, Russia, and Europe, and the rabbit shows him how and why people everywhere are being exploited (except in Russia, of course). After completing the trip, Hans returns with some bread for his mother and a great deal of knowledge of how capitalism functions. Balázs adapted the novel for the theater as a musical comedy with lyrics written by Eric Kästner and jazz music by Wilhelm Grosz. His rendition tended to sharpen the politically didactic message of the novel and provide a livelier dramatic plot.

Balázs's work on this fairy-tale play revealed to what extent he had become politicized by 1929 and how much he wanted to demonstrate his dedication to communism. His fairy tales had generally been much more philosophical and mystical than the play, and though they explored the need to overcome alienation, solitude, and oppression, they usually ended on a tragic or nostalgic note. They were not as hopeful as *Hans Urian*, which, of course, could be distinguished from his fairy tales written for adults. Balázs was, however, to return to sophisticated symbolism and intriguing mysticism soon after his work on this children's play. But in the spring of 1930 he suffered a heart attack on an outing in the countryside with Anna and had to be hospitalized for three months. During this period, while still in the hospital, he finished correcting the proofs for his second major book on film, *Geist des Films* (The Spirit of the Film), and in August, soon after he was released from the hospital, he became involved in another screenwriting debacle.

An argument between the eminent director Georg Pabst and the radical dramatist Bertolt Brecht and gifted musician Kurt Weill about the appropriate adaptation of Brecht's successful play *Die Dreigroschenoper* (The Three-Penny Opera, 1929) threatened to undermine the project.

Balázs was called upon to settle the dispute by writing a new screenplay. Brecht, who had retained the rights to approve the scenario, did not think highly of Balázs, and even though Balázs produced a screenplay that incorporated some of Brecht's and Pabst's ideas that served as the basis for the film, Brecht was dissatisfied and began suing Pabst and the Nero Film Company. In the meantime, Balázs, in need of rest after his heart attack, was fortunate to receive an offer to write a screenplay called *Die Löwin* (The Lioness), which was to be filmed in Algeria, where he could work and relax at the same time. Unfortunately, this film never saw the light of day owing to its anticolonialist tendencies. The French government confiscated it, and the film was never found. But Balázs managed to convalesce in Algeria.

In the spring of 1931, he was once again in Berlin and received a tempting offer to work on a film that he could not possibly refuse. The offer was made by the glamorous actress Leni Riefenstahl, who had not yet become notorious for her Nazi leanings, or perhaps through her producer Harry Sokal, to write the scenario for a mountain film, *Das blaue Licht* (The Blue Light), based on a Swiss novel. Riefenstahl, who by this time was twenty-eight and a star, wanted to direct the film and play the major role. Mountain films and novels had become very popular in Germany, even though they had been criticized by left-wing critics such as Siegfried Kracauer as representing the spirit of Nazism and idealizing nature and peasant life.[20] Balázs, who had spent part of his childhood in the mountains of Hungary, loved to hike, still clung to pantheism, and felt a special attachment to peasant life, disagreed with Marxist critics and defended the mountain films. Moreover, the opportunity to work with Riefenstahl and the great cameraman Hans Schneeberger was very appealing.

The plot of *The Blue Light*, which resembles both a legend and a fairy tale, is very simple. A young German painter by the name of Vigo appears in a small village in the Italian Dolomites to spend his summer vacation. He soon learns that there is a mysterious blue light that radiates from Monte Cristallo only at full moon and causes the superstitious villagers to close the shutters of their homes. He is then told that the magic power of the blue light attracts young men of the village and lures them to scale the summit of Monte Cristallo to find the source of the glowing light. Inevitably, they fall to their death, and strange statues in their memory are erected in the village. When Junta, a beautiful young peasant woman, always dressed in rags, appears in the village to sell some berries, the villagers begin to throw stones at her and chase her away. Only Vigo comes to her aid as she safely disappears into the mountains where she lives as an outcast. Later, Vigo learns that she is the only one who knows the source of the blue light and thus is blamed for the death of the young men and regarded as the devil's witch. Enchanted by her beauty, Vigo decides to wander into the mountains the next day and encounters Junta. They fall in love, and he dreams of spending the rest of his days in the mountains with her. After a few weeks pass, he follows her one night to the source of the blue light on top of Monte Cristallo and discovers a cave filled with glistening blue crystals. She does not realize that he has followed her, and the next day he descends into the village to tell the people about the crystals, for he believes that the crystals could make them and Junta rich and improve their living conditions. The villagers follow him to the cave and strip it of its beautiful crystals. That night they celebrate in a drunken revelry and keep Vigo with them. The next day he wants to return to his beloved Junta, but to his dismay, he finds her dead. She had discovered that the cave, which had been her temple, had been destroyed by the very people who had despised her. In despair, feeling violated, she had probably fallen to her death or committed suicide. Vigo is left alone and desolate.

Whether Balázs was responsible for the entire scenario of the film, or whether it was wholly Riefenstahl's work, as she later claimed, is a matter of debate. However, it is clear that Balázs spent a great deal of time developing the screenplay and even went to the Dolomites to help Riefenstahl direct the film. Several critics have interpreted the film as a protofascist celebration of the purity of nature and the violation of the innocent German woman, anticipating Riefenstahl's attraction to Hitler and Nazi mythology. On the other hand, Loewy and Zsuffa argue that Riefenstahl had been influenced by Balázs's leftist views, and one could interpret the film as anticapitalist and antireligious. It is certainly filled with pantheistic mysticism. There is hardly any dialogue in this film, and the close-ups of the leading characters and the different groups of villagers and their expressions speak volumes. The villagers are largely depicted as bitter, close-minded, disturbed, irrational, and violent. The priests and the elderly women are particularly mean and distasteful. Junta is desperate, fearful, innocent, good-natured, and isolated. She represents the misunderstood outsider, the eternal marginalized and alienated individual who lives in solitude. Vigo, the creative artist, is the only person who has empathy for her. He intuitively senses her innocence, which is associated with the majesty of pure nature, and how she is innately part and parcel of nature. She stands outside the norms and laws of society and does not need them. She is part of the blue light that recalls the German romantic poet Novalis's "Blue Flower," the symbol of eternal yearning and utopia. Vigo and Junta do not, however, speak the same language. She speaks an Italian dialect, and he speaks high German. Lacking verbal communication, they cannot articulate fully what each wants. Therefore, Vigo, thinking that he will do Junta good by leading the villagers to the cavern so that she might not be treated as a demonic outsider, does not appreciate her soulful dedication to the blue crystals. Her dreams and values are destroyed by miscommunication and greed. Certainly, if one interprets the film as a depiction of materialist greed, ignorance, and the destruction of ideals, one can see Balázs's imprint all over it—in the photographic close-ups of the expressions on people's faces and the mystical and majestic mountain as well as in the yearning and solitude of the distressed artist, who senses that he has brought about the death of his own dream.

As *The Blue Light* went into production, Balázs, who had joined the German Communist Party in the spring of 1931, was invited to Moscow to write a screenplay about the short-lived Hungarian Soviet Republic based on the novel *Tisza Gari* (The Tisza Burns), written by Béla Illés with an introduction by Béla Kun. Although internal disputes with Hungarian Communist Party members caused this project to be delayed and eventually to fail, Balázs decided that he would be better-off remaining in the Soviet Union to write and develop the projects that interested him, especially since the Nazis were gaining more power and he had cut most of his ties with the major German film studios.

In Moscow he and Anna began learning Russian while Balázs worked for different journals and tried to make contacts with important people in the Soviet film industry. The first three years in Moscow were extremely difficult. Though Balázs received an offer to teach film at the New School for Social Research in New York, which might have afforded him a more secure living, he rejected it out of dedication to the communist cause. Fortunately, his practical expertise in film enabled him to establish and support himself as a director and scenarist from 1932 to 1937. He advised film companies on how to adapt literary works for the cinema, and Ukrainfilm in Odessa placed him in charge of a propaganda film, *Karcsi kalandjai* (Hold Out, Charlie!), intended for children, that he had proposed. It had been clear to Balázs by 1933 that he could not return to Berlin after Hitler's seizure of power, nor could he return to Hungary. But even his security in Moscow was uncertain in 1935 because of the intrigues among the Hungarian and German communists and the tight control of the paranoid Stalinist government. The publication of a Russian translation of *The Spirit of the Film* caused consternation among Russian critics because it did not follow party cultural policy. Nevertheless, Balázs was able to defend his position and continue work on *Hold Out, Charlie!*; he also negotiated contracts to write a book about the theory of film and, in 1936, a play about Mozart for the Central Children's Theater in Moscow. The enterprising Balázs, often helped by his former wife Edith in Russia and in Europe, never lacked for projects, although many were rejected or never completed, and he lived in fear that he might be arrested and sent to a concentration camp.

In 1937 the Moscow show trials began, and most of the Hungarian Communist Party leadership, including Béla Kun, was executed. Numerous dedicated communists who had fled from Germany, Austria, and France were tried on false pretenses and murdered or sent to concentration camps. Balázs's younger brother, Ervin Bauer, who had become a renowned professor of biology at the University of Leningrad, was arrested that same year and sent to a gulag where he eventually died. Balázs ignominiously denied having any contact with him prior to the arrest and declared his allegiance to the Soviet government by writing letters to the Central Executive Committee of the USSR and the German section of the Comintern. To avoid the intrigues and possible persecution in Moscow, Balázs and Anna moved outside the city to the town of Istra, where they bought a cottage. Balázs hoped to live in solitude and focus mainly on his writing projects.

In 1938 he joined Lukács as one of the contributing editors of *Új Hang* (New Voice), a literary journal founded by Hungarian immigrants, and he continued to write for German publications while producing stories for children. However, since he did not toe the party line and had great difficulty in writing socialist realist fiction, he could never avoid conflict. During 1939, the year of the Hitler-Stalin pact, Balázs had a falling out with Lukács in the pages of the journal *Internationale Literatur*. Their estrangement had been growing since their emigration to the Soviet Union in 1932, and their friendship ended with a dispute about aesthetics and politics in which Balázs condemned the orthodox Marxist critiques made by Lukács, who had castigated Balázs for his expressionist and aesthetic approach to literature. In the meantime, Balázs began contemplating a new project that appeared to summarize his situation at the end of 1940. In a letter to the Committee on Art Affairs, he stated that he wanted to write about the eternal wandering Jew. As Zsuffa explains, Balázs declared that his eternal Jew would have

> "nothing in common with the original legend of the eternal Jew," who was condemned to keep wandering forever because he had driven Christ away from his doorstep. In Balázs's projected drama "the eternal Jew with the fall of Jerusalem, with the Diaspora, has lost his nation, his people. Since then, uprooted, he wanders restlessly throughout the world and seeks incarnation in folk and nation. As the bloodless shadows of the underworld thirst for blood, so does he thirst for materialization in the national life of a people, reaching down to the deep unconsciousness." Balázs's drama would take place not in the ancient but in modern times. In the problems and conflicts of this eternal Jew, all the ideological questions that influence present history and mobilize philosophies and tales would be reflections: "Nationalism or internationalism? Conservative tradition or revolutionary upheaval? Determination through the past or determination through the goal of the future? ... Taking root in the national soil or world horizon?" Balázs's hero would find the solutions to these dilemmas in the classless society of Communism, where he would experience no contradiction between national and international feelings.

There the wandering Jew could settle down and die at last in peace.[21]

Balázs, who clearly identified with the protagonist of his proposed play, was never able to develop this drama, nor did his own life lead to a happy end in a classless society. In December of 1941, he and Anna were forced to evacuate their cottage outside Moscow because the German troops were threatening devastation of the city. They were sent to Alma-Ata, capital of the Kazakh Soviet Republic in Central Asia, where they were to spend the next two years. During this time he and Anna contracted typhus, and Anna almost died. Balázs continued to work on two different screenplays and also took an interest in Kazakh folklore. He wrote an essay about the folktales and translated some narratives and poetry into German; they were published posthumously in *Das goldene Zelt: Kasachische Volksepen und Märchen* (The Golden Tent: Kazakhian Folk Epics and Fairy Tales) in 1956.

At the end of 1944 Balázs returned to Moscow, where he continued to make proposals for films dealing with the Nazis and World War II. When the war ended in the spring of 1945, his work and welcome in Moscow came to an end. Balázs was ceremoniously returned to Budapest by the Russian military in a plane after twenty-six years of exile. Now famous as a film theorist and screenplay writer, he hoped that he would become the director of a film institute or receive a professorship at the university. However, in part due to the animosity of Lukács, who played a major role in the cultural politics of postwar Hungary, Balázs was offered only a minor position as a lecturer at the newly founded film institute. Many other Hungarian communists suspected Balázs of betraying those Hungarian communists executed in Moscow and kept their distance from him. Despite the lack of recognition and support, Balázs was as active, idealistic, and ambitious as ever. His reputation grew in Europe through the publication of his autobiography, *Jugend eines Träumers* (The Youth of a Dreamer, 1946) and translations of *The Spirit of the Film* into different European languages. At the same time he resumed publishing in Hungarian with a volume of poetry *Az én utam* (My Road, 1945), translated *The Cloak of Dreams* (1948), and wrote the play *Cinka Panna Balladája* (The Ballad of Panna Cinka, 1948) with music by Kodály. This drama featured a wild female gypsy violinist, who leads a rebel army in the eighteenth century against Hapsburgs, and it bordered on fantastical mysticism that was not well received in postwar Hungary. Needless to say, the play was a flop, and Balázs was viciously attacked in the press and by party officials. Marginalized in Budapest, Balázs was a celebrated figure outside Hungary. He was continually invited to lecture on film in Italy, Poland, Austria, Czechoslovakia, and Germany and to attend film festivals. Toward the end of his life, he was negotiating with Deutsche Film A.G. (better known as DEFA) in East Berlin to become a major film consultant, which would have allowed him to spend more time in Germany, where he was more appreciated than in Hungary. However, he became ill and died from a brain hemorrhage in Budapest on May 20, 1949.

■

Balázs regarded himself as a man who lives on a borderline, as a wanderer, as a questioner. His approach to theory remained associative, dialogical, and essayistic—naive in an elementary sense. He clung tightly to the romantic notion of pan-symbolism through all the twists and turns of his way that transformed humans and things into forms of relationships in which transcendence and immanence are not separated from one another and vice versa. He attempted to secure and renew this permeability through a continual connection to a border realm between life and death and a temporary and suspended condition, that "other condition" in which artist as well as recipient was to experience the primary formation of symbol with deep pleasure.
—*Hanno Loewy*, Béla Balázs—Märchen, Ritual und Film[22]

Although it may appear as though Balázs wrote the sixteen "Chinese" fairy tales in *The Cloak of Dreams* in 1921 on a whim in response to a challenge and without preparation, nothing could be further from the truth. If anything, this book, his first major publication in German, represents the culmination of his interest in Asian art and the high point in his development as a writer of fairy tales. As Thomas Mann suggested in his review of the book, Balázs captured something of the Taoist Chinese spirit in these stories.[23]

It is difficult to establish exactly when Balázs began taking an interest in Asian art and culture because he read so voraciously and widely as a young man, but he was certainly acquainted with Chinese literature and art when he joined the Theosophical Society in 1914. It was about this time that he wrote an article "On the Philosophy of East Asian Art," in which he remarked:

> Chinese tales are full of the motif that statues converse and drink wine with humans. People suddenly find themselves *in* a picture, live in it for a few years with a painted woman and then come out of it, but since this visit the girl has put a kerchief over her hair, for she has become a woman!
>
> Pygmalion prayed to the gods to bring his sculpture to life. The Chinese artists pray lest their works grow alive, for they do not depict nature in dead pictures, but create new creatures already alive, increasing this way the number of the creatures of nature . . . for Chinese art is not symbolic. A picture or statue means only itself and nothing else.[24]

In fact, Balázs had already begun experimenting with his notions of Chinese literature, especially Taoist tales, sometime between 1908 and 1914, when he began publishing stories in *Nyugat*. One of his fairy tales, "Wan-Hu Csen könyve" ("The Book of Wan Hu-Chen"), is a good example. (See appendix B.) It was more than likely being written about this time and was published in Hungarian in *Seven Fairy Tales* in 1918 and later in German in 1921, several months before he received the commission to write his Chinese tales for Mariette Lydis. This tale is highly significant because it not only anticipates many of the themes in *The Cloak of Dreams* but also indicates just how integral Taoism had become to Balázs's personal philosophy.

"The Book of Wan Hu-Chen" recounts the strange life of Wan Hu-Chen, who wastes away the inheritance left to him by his parents and offends his wealthy relatives by reading books and studying for the state examination so that he can become a civil servant. He has no desire to do an honest day's work as a sailor, weaver, or merchant. However, Wan Hu-Chen is dumb. He fails the exams and gradually becomes so poor that his relatives mock him and cut him off from the family. In the meantime, Wan Hu-Chen falls in love with Li-Fan, the beautiful daughter of the governor of the region. Yet she has nothing but disdain for him. So poor Wan Hu-Chen wanders about during the day, scorned by society, and out of despair he begins writing a book about his unrequited love. At one point, he summons his fictional Li-Fan from the valley of the white apple blossoms to complain about her neglect of him. Gradually, after a major conflict, his imaginative world blends with his real world. As he turns older and has a child with the imagined Li-Fan, he decides to travel to the realm of the white apple blossoms and disappears from the earth. That is, he transcends earth through the ecstasy of love.

In many respects this tale could be considered very similar to a classical Taoist story. The themes of transformation, spiritual awakening, reincarnation, and regeneration are in keeping with Taoist philosophy. In addition, Balázs explores a variation on some of his usual themes in this unusual fairy tale: the marginalized writer, suffering in solitude, unrequited love, and commitment to the imagination and art as the means to personal fulfillment. Tao means the path or the way along which all things move, and unlike Western thinking, Taoism regards all matter as possessing spirit, and knowing as a form of noetic intuition. To learn how to go with the flow in life and become at one with all things is a key principle of Taoism. Simple as this may seem, it is not easy to discard rational thinking and illusion and attain oneness with nature. As Raymond Van Over explains,

> To understand the Tao one must first realize that the heavenly Tao simply pursues its course and does not speak about it or synthesize its essence: So, says the

Taoist, let human action be like water that quietly seeks out all the crevices of life, but it does it silently and effortlessly. If resistance is met, it is best to rest passively until it is exhausted and then go on one's way. In other words, he who is completely identified with the course of nature flows effortlessly with it, never fighting or resisting such infinite power but utilizing its strength for one's own fulfillment. . . . In psychological terms this implies the destruction of arrogance, egotism, and desire—of the restless spirit that seeks to conquer and serve its own ends. To accomplish effortlessly is the virtue of natural man—the man who has Tao.[25]

Certainly, Balázs did not have Tao and never became a Taoist, but his inclination toward Taoism was evident in his early leanings toward pantheism, mysticism, and romanticism and in his writings. In "The Aesthetics of Death," the essay he wrote for Simmel's seminar in 1907, there is strong indication of how close his thinking was to Taoism. "Art," he wrote, "is the perception of the transcendence of life. In other words, art is the consciousness of life. . . . The consciousness of life depends on death, in other words, art depends on death."[26]

The paradox of death giving birth to life through artistic form is central to understanding why the fairy tale became so important to Balázs and remained essential for him throughout his life. Loewy remarks that "at the high point of his 'Aesthetics of Death' Balázs turned quickly away from the tragedy and to the fairy tale, and this deserves special attention. For him, the fairy tale embodies a special paradox and at the same time the greatest opposite imaginable to the 'religious art' of the tragedy. Where the connection with death or the tragic contradiction leads to the *highest* consciousness, the fairy tale, as art of the folk, leads away into a flat world of unconsciousness, into a world in which nothing is impossible."[27]

Many currents of thought intersect in Balázs's conception of the fairy tale, and they include the theoretical influences of Simmel and Lukács. In the end, however, his notion of the fairy tale as folk art in which nothing is impossible remained peculiarly his own, for his personal philosophy was embedded in it as were his experiences. When Balázs began writing the fairy tales of *The Cloak of Dreams*, he was thirty-seven years old. He had lost his father as a boy; moved from a provincial city to Budapest as a poor but talented student; participated in the Hungarian cultural renaissance at the beginning of the twentieth century by writing poems, stories, librettos, essays, reviews, and plays; formed a mutually beneficial friendship with Lukács; traveled in Austria, Germany, and France; married a wealthy and gifted Hungarian woman; converted to Catholicism out of convenience; fought as a common soldier in World War I; divorced and married another woman, who had left her husband for him; took part in the Hungarian communist revolution; fought in the Red Army; escaped to Vienna with his second wife; barely made a living; and began writing in his mother tongue, German, knowing that his life would depend on his ability to communicate in a language that was in some ways foreign to him.

Throughout his life Balázs yearned of returning to the folk and becoming one with an idealized classless society in which he would be accepted. Did he want to return to the Hungarian community from which he felt excluded? Or did he want to gain a sense of his Jewish roots, which had never been adequately planted? The answer is not clear, but the medium he employed to express his feelings of marginalization and his yearning for communion and community was the fairy tale, whether in the form of prose narrative, drama, libretto, children's story, film, or poem.

There is some evidence that Balázs may have read a collection of Chinese novellas and stories in preparation for writing the collection of tales for Mariette Lydis's paintings. Lee Congdon states: "In order to produce the book by Christmas, the publisher asked to have the stories in hand within three weeks. After some financial haggling, Balázs accepted the assignment and, having perused a volume of Chinese fables to get a feel for the 'jargon,' set to work."[28] Congdon does not cite his source, but Balázs might have read one of the following three books: Leo Greiner's *Chinesische Abende: Novellen und Geschichten* (Chinese Evenings: Novellas and Stories, 1913), Paul Kühnel's *Chinesische Novellen* (Chinese Novellas, 1914), or Hans Rudelsberger's *Chinesische Novellen* (Chinese Novellas, 1914). All three works underwent several printings and would have been available to Balázs, and all three would have provided models that might have inspired him. They contain stories from the oral and literary traditions of China that date back to the first century and reveal a great deal about Chinese customs and thinking. All three authors translated the tales, employing a restrained and succinct style in German that contrasted with the unusual contents: extraordinary incidents in worlds in which everything was constantly alive and being transformed and reincarnated.

The tales in *The Cloak of Dreams* are stunning because Balázs managed to interpret the paintings of Mariette Lydis in keeping with various strands of Taoist and Confucian philosophy while drawing associations from his own personal experiences. Like Hermann Hesse, who was writing fairy tales influenced by Asian thinking at the same time, Balázs drew inspiration and hope from tales of transformation, even when many end sadly, tragically, and nostalgically. It is interesting to note that the two tales that "encase" the collection, "The Cloak of Dreams" and "The Victor," concern alienation and suicide. There is something very sad about the empress Nai-Fe, who can only keep her vows of love to her husband by gazing at the images of her dreams that she herself has stitched into his cloak. There is something equally heartrending about the general Du-Dsi-Tsun, who maims opponents in his quest to find the love of a woman and tenderness and then kills himself out of shame. Balázs thrives on paradoxes, mystery, and mysticism. His terse, simple prose veils the complexity of his metaphysical thought and the connections to his own life.

Many of his tales are reflections of friendship and the hardship one must endure to maintain a true relationship and understand its profound significance. Balázs suffered a great deal in his friendship with Lukács as well as with other men, such as Bartók and Kodály, and there are obvious references to his sentiments about these friendships, or lack of understanding, in his depictions of friends in "The Clumsy God," "The Opium Smokers," and "The Friends." In the latter tale, Balázs portrayed an ideal relationship, perhaps one that he envisioned with Lukács and could never realize in his personal dealings with the impervious philosopher. The marginalized friends become gods celebrated for their devotion to one another and the principles of friendship they exemplify. The meaning of friendship is expressed through their actions and behavior, not through words. Balázs sought to make his tales come alive, part of life, at one with the images and his readers.

To read Balázs's fairy tales is to *experience* the bitterness and joys of life and to reach a condition of suspension or liminality in which nothing can be explained rationally but everything can be understood intuitively. In tales such as "The Parasols," "The Flea," "The Old Child," "Li-Tai-Pe and Springtime," "The Moon Fish," and "Tearful Gaze," the characters are transformed and find their paths to self-fulfillment by following their intuition or being inspired by their imaginations. Nothing is impossible in these fairy tales because the protagonists learn to overcome the duality between the real and spiritual worlds. In "Li-Tai-Pe and Springtime" the poet learns that "knowing is happiness and happiness is knowing" by recognizing that he must penetrate the superficial side of beautiful nature and by grasping its spiritual and physical wholeness.

Evil in Balázs's fairy tales is manifested through greed and lust for power that result in warrantless killing. In "The Robbers of Divine Power," the images of the band of brutal warriors and the devastation they cause evoke the barbarism of World War I. The marauders do not disappear from earth but continue to exist, as Balázs suggests, and can erupt at any time. In "The Revenge of the Chestnut Tree," another robber is haunted by nature because of his unnatural or perverse use of his power. Nature takes its revenge through its mysterious transformative power, and he dies in the same way that he has brutally lived and ravaged other people.

Perhaps the most curious, autobiographical, and chilling of Balázs's tales is "The Ancestors." A customs officer, content with his life, is driven to his death by the demands of three dead skulls—his father, grandfather, and great-grandfather—who want him to fulfill their destinies. In the gruesome ending—they devour him after he dies—Balázs reckons with tradition and the past. As a young writer at the beginning of the twentieth century, he belonged to the cultural movement of young intellectuals who resisted the past or wanted to rejuvenate the past in their own terms, invigorating Hungarian culture. Though he was a published author and well known in Budapest's cultural circles, Balázs's neoromantic and mystical writings were also heavily attacked by the old guard and traditionalists. Chased out of Budapest by the White Army after the revolution, Balázs was exhausted and desperate in 1919. His past had caught up to him, but unlike the pathetic customs officer in his story, Balázs did not allow himself to be torn apart. By this time he had faith in a different past that was to be his future, namely, his devotion to communism.

Unfortunately, or fortunately, Balázs was never able to reconcile his art with communism. *The Cloak of Dreams*, though filled with class antagonism and critiques of materialism, are not "socialist" fairy tales per se, which he would write after he settled in Vienna and Berlin. His Chinese tales are more a blend of romantic anticapitalist and Taoist notions about optional paths and alternative ways of life. It is easy to see, despite their provocative and disturbing endings, how these fairy tales may have brought Balázs some joy and comfort. It was through transforming the fairy tale that he could depict the possibilities of life under impossible conditions. Balázs's radical contribution to the modern fairy tale was to demonstrate what the great German romantic Novalis had written more than a hundred years ago: we can only learn to become true human beings through art.

Unless otherwise indicated, all the translations in the introduction are my own.

1 Cited in Béla Balázs, *Der heilige Räuber und andere Märchen*, ed. Hanno Loewy (Berlin: Arsenal, 2005), 185.

2 Joseph Zsuffa, *Béla Balázs: The Man and the Artist* (Berkeley: University of California Press, 1987), xi. Aside from Zsuffa's excellent biography, see also the important essay by Tibor Frank, "Béla Balázs: From the Aesthetization of Community to the Communization of the Aesthetic," *Journal of the Interdisciplinary Crossroads*, 3.1 (2006): 117–34.

3 Quoted in Lee Congdon, *Exile and Social Thought: Hungarian Intellectuals in Germany and Austria, 1919–1933* (Princeton: Princeton University Press, 1991), 101. Sándor Petöfi (1823–1849) was a Magyar of Slovak descent.

4 Hanno Loewy, *Béla Balázs—Märchen, Ritual und Film* (Berlin: Vorwerk 8, 2003), 10–11.

5 Béla Balázs, "Todesästhetik," trans. Anna Bak-Gara and Marina Gschmeidler, *Mitteilungen des Filmarchiv Austria* 2 (2004): 68–69.

6 Ferenc Fehér, "Das Bündnis von Georg Lukács und Béla Balázs bis zur ungarischen Revolution," in *Die Seele und das Leben: Studien zum frühen Lukács*, ed. Agnes Heller et al. (Frankfurt am Main: Suhrkamp, 1977), 145.

7 See Aranka Ugrin and Kálmán Vargha, eds., *"Nyugat" und sein Kreis, 1908–1944* (Leipzig: Philip Reclam, 1989).

8 For two excellent studies of this friendship, see Fehér, "Das Bündnis von Georg Lukács und Béla Balázs bis zur ungarischen Revolution," 131–76, and Júlia Lenkei, "Béla Balázs

and György Lukács: Their Contacts in Youth," in *Hungarian Studies on György Lukács*, ed. László Illés (Budapest: Akadémiai Kiadó, 1993), 1:66–86.

9 For a thorough treatment of the opera, see Carl Leafstedt, *Inside Bluebeard's Castle: Music and Drama in Béla Bartók's Opera* (New York: Oxford University Press, 1999).

10 Fehér, "Das Bündnis von Georg Lukács und Béla Balázs bis zur ungarischen Revolution," 165.

11 Béla Balázs, *Sieben Märchen*, trans. Elsa Stephani (Vienna: Rikola, 1921), 51.

12 Zsuffa, *Béla Balázs: The Man and the Artist*, 52–53.

13 For a full account of the Sunday Circle, see Éva Karádi and Erzsébet Vezér, eds., *Georg Lukács, Karl Mannheim und der Sonntagskreis*, trans. Albrecht Friedrich (Frankfurt am Main: Sendler, 1985).

14 Georg Lukács, *Balázs Béla és akiknek nem kell* (Gyoma: Kner, 1918). This book has not been translated.

15 In Lenkei, "Béla Balázs and György Lukács," 76.

16 Quoted in Congdon, *Exile and Social Thought*, 103.

17 Mariette Lydis was actually an Austrian of Greek descent. Her maiden name was Ronsperger, and she was born in Vienna in 1887. In 1925 she went to Paris, where she made a name for herself, and then emigrated to South America in 1940. She died in Buenos Aires in 1970. See the note on the illustrator for more information.

18 Loewy, *Béla Balázs—Märchen, Ritual und Film*, 12–13.

19 See Congdon, *Exile and Social Thought*, 109–16.

20 See the discussions about this film in John Ralmon, "Béla Balázs in German Exile," *Film Quarterly* 30.3 (1977): 12–19;

Zsuffa, *Béla Balázs: The Man and the Artist*, 217–40; and Loewy, *Béla Balázs—Märchen, Ritual und Film*, 352–78.

21 Zsuffa, *Béla Balázs: The Man and the Artist*, 297–98.

22 Loewy, *Béla Balázs—Märchen, Ritual und Film*, 12.

23 Thomas Mann, "Ein schönes Buch," *Neue Freie Presse* (March 1, 1922). See appendix A.

24 In Lenkei, "Béla Balázs and György Lukács," 82.

25 Raymond Van Over, ed., *Taoist Tales* (New York: Signet, 1973), 7–8.

26 In Lenkei, "Béla Balázs and György Lukács," 74.

27 Loewy, *Béla Balázs—Märchen, Ritual und Film*, 34. Loewy quotes extensively from Balázs's "The Aesthetics of Death" in this paragraph.

28 Congdon, *Exile and Social Thought*, 104.

Most of the publications of *The Cloak of Dreams* in German, Italian, and English and the biographies of Béla Balázs refer to Mariette Lydis as a Greek millionaire and painter and merely give her birth and death dates, or they do not refer to her at all. In fact, Mariette Lydis was a gifted painter and illustrator, whose adventurous life and accomplishments are worth a book.

She was born in Baden, near Vienna, as Marietta Ronsperger on August 24, 1887. Very little is known of her youth, for she was reluctant to write about her personal life. Nevertheless, some biographical details are verifiable. She came from a well-to-do family and was close to her mother. Evidently, she was self-educated as an artist, and though she disliked traveling, she lived in or visited Germany, Russia, Turkey, Morocco, Greece, Switzerland, Italy, France, and England during the early part of the twentieth century. After marrying Jean Lydis in 1920, she moved to a small city outside Athens around 1922. A few years later, she left her husband, and while living near Florence, she met the popular Italian writer Massimo Bontempelli and began an affair. In 1925 she traveled to France with Bontempelli, who introduced her to intellectual and artistic circles in Paris. Within a few years, Lydis established a name for herself and was reputed to be a talented painter, engraver, and illustrator. In 1928 she had an affair with Joseph Delteil and illustrated one of his books, *Le petit Jésus*. That same year she began another affair with the art publisher of Les Presses de l'Hotel Sagonne, Comte Giuseppe Govone, and married him on August 1, 1934. While in Paris, Lydis continued to have great success as an artist. She became a member and juror of the Salon d'Autonne and had a solo exhibit at the Galerie Bernheim Jeune. She also illustrated numerous books by French authors, including Henry de Montherlant, Paul Valéry, Pierre Louÿs, Paul Verlaine, and Jules Superveille. In particular, she was a close friend of Montherlant, who edited a book of her illustrations and paintings in 1949.[29] By 1937 she had left her husband and was involved in an affair with Erika Marx, her editor at Les Presses de l'Hotel Sagonne. In August of 1939, they fled the Nazis and made their way to Winchcombe, a small village near London, where Lydis was able to work and prepare an exhibit to be held in Buenos Aires. Then, in September of 1940, Lydis embarked for Buenos Aires and decided to remain there owing to her fear of bombardments and a possible German invasion of England. Alone at first, Lydis soon formed friendships and became active as a painter and illustrator. After World War II her husband, Giuseppe Govone, joined her in Buenos Aires, where he established himself briefly as a publisher and produced some of her works. By 1948, however, they decided to return to Paris, and shortly after their return, Govone died in Milan. For the next few years Lydis remained in Paris and continued to work for numerous French publishers and illustrated books by Guy de Maupassant, Colette, Baudelaire, Rimbaud, and Bella Moerel as well as *The Turn of the Screw* by Henry James. Lydis is said to have had a close relationship with the aviator Amelia Earhart about this time. Concerned about the threat of another war in Europe, she returned to Buenos Aires in the early 1950s but retained most of her contacts with publishers and writers in Paris. She continued to reside in Buenos Aires until her death on April 26, 1970.

It is not known when or where she studied art in Vienna during her youth, if she studied at an academy at all, for she stated in an autobiographical introduction, "Coupe à travers moi-même," that she was self-taught.[30] Neither is it known whether her Chinese aquarelles have survived. Significantly, *The Cloak of Dreams* was the first book she illustrated, that is, it was the first book in which her paintings appeared as illustrations. Soon after that publication, she provided the illustrations for *Miniaturen zum Koran* (Miniatures for the Koran, 1924) and wrote and illustrated an exotic book, *Orientalisches Traumbuch*

(Oriental Book of Dreams, 1925). These early works, which demonstrated her interest in the bizarre and the extraordinary, paved the way for her success in Paris and later in Buenos Aires. Several reports have indicated that she was influenced by the Japanese artist Tsuguharu Foujita, whom she met in Montmartre. Her paintings, prints, and illustrations reveal a flair for the erotic and demonstrate great nuance and delicacy. Montherlant stated that she "always pursued the other thing that was in each thing, the many things that are in each thing."[31] She herself wrote, "My first efforts—my first interests—were concentrated on portraying poor people, the old men, the dispossessed, the criminals, and the sick. I wanted to depict how much sadness there is in the world. . . . Later my vision became brighter. I began to see the beauty in softness, in candor, and this manifested itself in a number of drawings and paintings of women, adolescents, and children."[32] Throughout her career, she painted with an eye toward revealing the essence of the human condition. Working with pastels, charcoal, oil, and ink, she demonstrated a unique capacity to illustrate literary works and also to produce original portraits and still-life paintings. Always open-minded, she had a great interest in Asian art and surrealism. Many of her prints and illustrations deal with controversial topics and poses. In all respects, she was an avant-garde feminist who explored all aspects of art with great integrity and intrepidity.

NOTES

1 See Henry de Montherlant, *Mariette Lydis* (Bobigny, France: Nouvelles Éditions Françaises, 1949).

2 See *Mariette Lydis: 39 Reproductions en noir et 16 en coleur* (Buenos Aires: Viau, 1945). This book includes an introduction, "Coupe à travers moi-même" by Mariette Lydis, pp. 9–18.

3 Montherlant, *Mariette Lydis*, 6.

4 *Mariette Lydis: 39 Reproductions en noir et 16 en coleur*, 13–14.

The Cloak of Dreams

1 | The Cloak of Dreams

The emperor Ming-Huang, a descendant of the T'ang dynasty, had a wife named Nai-Fe, who was as beautiful as the moon in May. However, they were never seen conversing with one another, sitting together, or holding hands. His wife Nai-Fe only appeared when the emperor put on his marvelous embroidered cloak. Then she walked behind him, keeping a great distance between them, and the yearning of her soul rested on him with her gaze. Let me tell you how all this came about.

Ming-Huang had a glorious garden that had such a powerful fragrance you could fetch an aroma out of the garden with your bare hand like water from a spring. One time he stood with his empress in this garden on the seventh night of the week, and as they looked at the constellation of the weaver and the shepherd in the sky, they swore eternal love to one another.

But the empress Nai-Fe had a dreaming soul because she had died too early in her previous life. This is why her gaze always roamed far away, following her dreams, and carried her beyond her imperial husband. Even when he held her in his arms, her soul was very far from him. It was just like the spirit of someone sleeping that cannot be held down and flies away in the dream. This is why their love was damaged. Nai-Fe reproached herself bitterly, but she could do nothing about it.

One night, while she was sleeping in the gazebo made out of pale green jade and her bed was swaying on the fragrant waves like a boat on the back of a stream, she saw the emperor Ming-Huang. He was wearing a marvelous cloak on which all the images of her dreams had been embroidered—gigantic mountains with glistening cliffs and wide golden rivers, magical gardens and palaces, sweet fairies and wild dragons spitting fire. His cloak carried the entire dreamland for which her soul yearned. Nai-Fe's heart was delighted and filled with happiness, for now she could keep her gaze upon the emperor and hold it forever. No longer did she have to choose between the path of her dreams and the path of her love.

When Nai-Fe awakened from her sleep, she went to the emperor and said to him, "When we were standing that time on the seventh night of the week in the sweet-smelling garden and looked up at the constellation of the weaver and the shepherd, I swore eternal love to you. But I have a dreaming soul because I died too early in my previous life, and it diverts my gaze away from you. Our love has been damaged by this, and I can't keep the vow I made to you. Therefore, you must wear my dreams so that I can

gaze upon you when I look for my dreams, and when I pursue them, I'll come to you."

"How can I wear your dreams?" the emperor asked sadly.

"I shall embroider them all in a cloak that you must wear."

The empress Nai-Fe went into the gazebo made out of pale green jade, and for five long years she embroidered a cloak. For five long years she did not leave the gazebo. Only the fragrance of the garden drifted toward her, and she sensed the change of seasons as the aromas changed. This was the way she could count the five years as they passed.

When Nai-Fe finished embroidering the cloak, she brought it to the emperor Ming-Huang, and he put it on. Her bosom was filled with joy and happiness because she saw the emperor wrapped in her dreams. She looked at him, and the yearning of her soul and the yearning of her heart burned in her eyes at the same time. Then Nai-Fe stretched out her arms and wanted to approach the emperor to rest her head on his chest. But she couldn't come close to him. The gigantic mountains with the glistening rocks blocked her way. The wide golden rivers blocked her way. The large magic gardens, the sweet fairies, and the wild dragons spitting fire were embroidered so artfully that they blocked the way of the empress. The entire, spacious dreamland lay between her and the emperor, and she couldn't come to him.

Suddenly tears streamed down her cheeks, and the emperor cried out, "I won't wear the cloak!"

Nai-Fe responded very sadly, "You must choose, Ming-Huang. If you take off the cloak, you can hold me in your arms, but my soul will be far away from you. If you wear the cloak, I won't be able to approach you, and I won't be able to come to you. But the longing of my soul will eternally cast its glances upon you. You must choose, but think about the vow we made on that seventh night and about the secret talks we had that nobody knows."

So the emperor Ming-Huang chose to wear the cloak of dreams. Since then, nobody has ever seen him together with his wife Nai-Fe, who was as beautiful as the moon in May. Only when he put on his embroidered cloak could one see Nai-Fe as well. She walked behind him, keeping a great distance, and the yearning of her soul rested on him with her gaze. ∎

The poet Li-Tai-Pe sang so gloriously that his songs intoxicated the gods above, and they often became inebriated and dropped to the earth from the clouds like little sleeping birds from their nest. This is why Li-Tai-Pe was so highly honored during his lifetime. Temples were built on mountain peaks in his honor. The emperor presented him with the most beautiful clothes, and the most beautiful empress undressed him. And when he stayed in a city, the men of this city would go looking for him with worried expressions on their faces, and they searched in all the gutters of the streets like mothers concerned that one of their children had gone astray. This was because Li-Tai-Pe loved wine too much and drank every night until he was intoxicated. He did this because he wanted to be inspired, and he had no other wings with which to fly from earth. So he drank until his head slumped, and the rim of his glass pressed red rings on his pale forehead.

One time Li-Tai-Pe received a hundred gold coins from the emperor for a song in which he had celebrated the stallion the emperor had ridden in times of war. After-

ward Li-Tai-Pe wandered through the country again and came to the city of Tsian-Hu, where he sat down under the evening stars and drank. His heart was filled with sadness because he thought he'd never find any inspiration, song, or wine capable of lifting him completely from earth. This was because the earth always pulled him back with its sharp hook of pain and sorrow. One time he fell and sprained his foot. Another time he saw a mistress he had left years ago in the arms of some uncouth warrior, or he caught sight of the poorly penciled eyebrows of the empress. Something always happened that lamed the wings of his intoxication.

"Today, I'm going to get so drunk," he cried out, "that no earthly trouble will bother me."

And Li-Tai-Pe sat in the city of Tsian-Hu under the stars and drank one glass after another. Soon he became inspired and sang:

"I have sowed the stars in the heavens,
And mine is the silver crescent of the moon.
And as the golden kernels of the stars ripen
into golden waving ears of stars
bearing twenty times more of glittering gold,
I shall mow them with the silver sickle of the moon."

As Li-Tai-Pe was singing this way, a thief came crawling toward him to steal his bag with the hundred gold coins from his pocket. But when Li-Tai-Pe caught sight of him and turned his head, the thief started to run away.

"Don't run away, my honorable thief," the enthused poet cried out. "The blessed intoxication has lifted me from earth. Mine will be the gold of all the future heavens, and truly, I don't care at all about the hundred gold coins in my pocket."

"My most honorable poet," said the thief, "you say that now in your intoxicated state, but if I were to take the gold coins from your pocket, your intoxication would be over, and you would turn me over to the police."

When Li-Tai-Pe heard this, tears welled up in his eyes, and he cried out:

"No, oh honorable thief, no! I beg of you, come and steal the gold from me. Otherwise I'll never have proof that this intoxication has really lifted me from earth. Please, dear thief, please, my highly honorable thief, my brother! Come and steal the emperor's gold coins."

As soon as the thief saw tears streaming down the pale cheeks of the poet, he finally believed him. So he went to the poet, reached under his arm, and stole the bag of coins from his pocket.

Li-Tai-Pe was happy and became even more intoxicated because of this. Having now attained what he wanted, he continued singing his song so gloriously that the gods above became drunk and fell from the clouds to the earth like little sleeping birds from their nest. ■

3 | The Parasols

There once lived a man by the name of Yang-Tsu. He was a peddler and spent the entire day wandering from street to street with a basket hanging from his chest. In this way he managed to see all the splendors of the rich city. He saw the magnificent mandarins with their retinues. He saw the powerful warriors with the shadows of distant adventures on their faces. And he felt the aroma of almonds coming from the invisible ladies in the veiled, gilt-embroidered sedan chairs that smacked him in his sweaty face.

In the evening, however, when he returned home to his wife Yu-Nu, he squabbled with her, for he was restless and excited. Then there were tears and complaints throughout the night.

One morning his wife Yu-Nu awoke once again with her eyes red from crying. When she noticed this in the mirror, she said to Yang-Tsu, "Go and buy yourself a parasol."

"Why should I go and buy myself a parasol?" her husband asked irritably.

"Because the heat of the sun is the cause of it all. The strong rays of the sun make you irritable, and that's why you squabble. That's why we're unhappy, and my eyes become red from crying."

Yang-Tsu went off to do his daily chores without responding. He wasn't a bad man, and he took his wife's words to heart. When he was now out on the streets, the sun shone so strongly that its rays stood straight up on the cobblestones like the bars of a glowing golden grating. "Perhaps she's right," Yang-Tsu thought, and he directed his steps toward the quarter where the artisans had their stalls.

There was a lot of noise and commotion in this quarter, because each man sat on a mat in front of his shop and praised his wares in a loud voice. Suddenly, Yang-Tsu heard a shrill voice arising from all the commotion, and it called out, "Parasols for sale! The greatest selection! Spread your most favorite sky over your head!"

Yang-Tsu was very much astounded by these strange words and went over to the parasol maker, who was a large and serious man. He sat on the cobblestones of the street, and all around him lay the parasols.

"What did you cry out, most honorable man?" Yang-Tsu addressed him. "Could these parasols spread a sky over my head? Certainly, I find them beautiful, but they aren't any different from the others that I've seen."

Then the parasol maker answered with a serious smile: "The other parasols seem to be similar from the outside, oh honorable one. But open these up."

Yang-Tsu lifted a parasol from the ground, opened it, and was immediately struck by astonishment. The interior of the parasol was painted with a summer sky full of soft curly clouds, and the images had been done so artistically that he felt as if he were wandering about under this sky.

"You see, most honorable one," said the parasol maker, "as long as you carry this parasol, the bright summer sky will never darken over your head, and your soul will always be cheerful under its influence."

Yang-Tsu was overjoyed, but he replied cautiously, "To be sure, I have every intention of buying a parasol because I squabble every night with my wife Yu-Nu. This is due to the summer heat. But I don't believe that a warm summer sky over my head will be able to calm me down."

"Choose another sky," the parasol maker said. "I own the largest selection of skies in the entire city."

And so Yang-Tsu opened another parasol. It was a plain cloudy winter sky that seemed to be made out of shimmering gray silk. The smoke of distant villages could be seen rising in the sky on the horizon.

"That's the sky of tender melancholy," the parasol maker said. "You would live your entire life peacefully in this melancholy as though you were wrapped in soft wool."

Yang-Tsu found the sky too gloomy and opened a third parasol and then a fourth, and he kept on looking. There was a morning sky right before sunrise in which all the days events glowed in their purity before they fell down to the besmirched earth. There was one in which he saw blue through the thicket of towering blades of grass as if he were lying on his back and looking up dreamily into the

sky. Under this parasol he could carry the deep peace of solitude with himself through all the noisy streets. There was another with a nocturnal sky. The full moon shone upon it, and all the songs of carousers and lovers hung on it like sweet grapes. There was a parasol with a crystal sky over snow-covered mountains where the soul was no longer disturbed by any sign of life.

Yang-Tsu chose the nocturnal sky with the full moon and went off. But the parasol did not bring peace into his house. The songs of the carousers and the lovers trickled from the moon down into his soul and filled him with passion so that he didn't feel at home with himself. On the third day Yang-Tsu carried the full-moon parasol back and exchanged it for the one with the quiet solitude of the meadows. However, this one did not do him any good either. He forgot to attend to his business too often, and whenever his wife merely spoke to him, he appeared to be startled out of a dream, and he felt bad. So he returned this parasol, too, on the third day. Gradually, he exchanged one parasol after the other, and soon he had tried them all.

Then the parasol maker said to Yang-Tsu: "You have now tried every sky, and none of them has calmed your soul so that you can live in peace with your wife. I have one more parasol left, and perhaps fate will determine that it will be of use to you."

The parasol maker placed his hands on his knees for support and coughed as he stood up, for he was a heavyset man. He went inside to his workshop and soon fetched a parasol that seemed less beautiful than the others. Yang-Tsu opened it and saw an autumn evening sky, gray and reddened on the horizon. Wild geese flew over him in a long wedge form. A painful yearning gripped his heart as he looked at the wild geese and followed their flight—a yearning for unknown, unreachable distant places. But Yang-Tsu took the parasol with him because he no longer had a choice.

With the autumn evening sky over his head and the distant, vague yearning in his heart, he wandered through the streets of the city and saw the splendor of the rich people, the magnificent mandarins, the powerful warriors, and the gilt-embroidered and veiled sedan chairs. However, none of this excited his soul any longer because his glance followed the wild geese toward unknown distant places. And when he returned home to his wife in the evening, he was somewhat melancholy, but he spoke to her in a quiet and friendly voice.

From that day on, Yang-Tsu lived peacefully and contentedly with his wife Yu-Nu. To be sure, they often had painful and turbulent feelings in their hearts just as many people do when their little homes are too small. Whenever that happened, they opened the parasol, looked at the flying geese, and followed their flight. Then their restlessness and yearning flew far away, carried by the geese just as smoke flows through the chimney and doesn't poison the room. Soon Yu-Nu no longer had red eyes from crying, and in time she became well nourished and plump. ■

Fu-Hi had been covered by a mountain for a thousand long years. This was how the Lord of the Heavens had punished him for his clumsiness.

It all began right after Fu-Hi's mortal death, when he was appointed god of friendship. He had not governed very long in his office and had not yet been registered in the imperial sacrificial lists when, one day, a golden dragon appeared before him as messenger and summoned him to the Lord of the Heavens. All at once clouds billowed from Fu-Hi's feet. Then he climbed upon them and flew past the nineteen houses of the moon and through the thirty-three heavens to the great alabaster throne, where the Lord of the Heavens was sitting and where golden dragons crawled through his ears and re-emerged through his nose.

"Fu-Hi," said the Lord of the Heavens, "you have been governing in your office for only a short time. You need some practical experience. Look down below: there is an old man standing at the River of the Seven Bends. His name is Chang-Be, and he is holding a burning torch in his hand and wants to set fire to his neighbor's house. Go there, and reconcile the two of them, for they are deeply bound to one another."

Fu-Hi was happy to have received such an assignment and flew as fast as he could through the thirty-three heavens and past the nineteen houses of the moon down to earth, where he assumed the guise of an old wise man and appeared before Chang-Be just as he was about to set fire to his neighbor's house.

"Stop!" he called out to him. "Don't harm your neighbor! Instead, I advise you to make up with him, for you are deeply bound to one another."

Old Chang-Be turned to the stranger and looked at him for a long time. Finally, he said, "You seem to be a learned man, for your eyebrows have a certain inclination. But what do you know about us? At one time during my youth my neighbor was my friend. However, there was a thorn between us, and the tighter we embraced one another, the deeper the thorn pierced our hearts. Until today I've never done anything to harm him. Now I am old and shall die very soon. But the knot of hatred shall be unraveled in this lifetime."

After he said all this, he raised the torch to light the straw beneath the roof of his neighbor's house.

"Stop!" Fu-Hi cried loudly, anxious that he might not succeed in carrying out his assignment. "I've come to announce to you that you will die today before the second change of the night watch. Go home, bring your house in order, and take a last look at the life that you've led. You will glimpse your future incarnation and see how deeply you are bound to your neighbor."

With these words Fu-Hi rose into the clouds, and Chang-Be realized that he had been speaking to a god who had come to announce his pending death. So old Chang-Be became pensive and put out the torch in the dust on the ground.

"If I am to die today," he said, "then it is of little use to open the festering tumor of hatred and to let the pus flow. I'd only disturb my neighbor and wouldn't have any time to reconcile myself with him."

Therefore, he went home and hid his precious things so that his nimble relatives would not be able to pocket them so quickly before the executor of his estate arrived. Then he wrote a conciliatory letter to his neighbor and went into the city to have a last look around. Fu-Hi had also arrived in the city and had hastily prepared a great miracle because he wanted be certain he had converted old Chang-Be. Indeed, he had been extremely afraid of failing the Lord of the Heavens.

First, old Chang-Be went to a theater and watched a play. Then he went to a teahouse. Afterward he listened to a street singer who sang "The Maiden's Lament" in a pleasant voice. When the time had arrived for the first change of the night watch, he went to the tents to see the strange exhibitions and freak shows. In one of the tents, Siamese twins were on display. The two of them shared just two

legs and two hands. Old Chang-Be entered this tent because he wanted to enjoy this rare show before he died.

The twins stood on a table, and the man who was exhibiting them stood nearby. As old Chang-Be moved closer, he realized that he himself was one of the twins, and the other, his neighbor. They had become attached to one another and had grown together.

Chang-Be was most astonished and asked the man who was exhibiting the twins all about this. In turn, the man replied, "You already know that you will die today. Now you can see how you will be reincarnated. Indeed, this is the way you'll spend your entire life, attached and growing together with your neighbor. This is why I advise you not to harm him but to reconcile yourself with him."

When old Chang-Be heard these words, he became pensive once again and left the tent with a bowed head. However, Fu-Hi—for the man who showed the twins was none other than the god—flew joyfully and contentedly to his post high up in the heavens, for he was convinced that he had carried out everything for the best.

Meanwhile, old Chang-Be went home, where he tore up the conciliatory letter. Then he fetched the torch and lit it.

"If I'm to be bound to my neighbor and grow together with him throughout my entire next life," he remarked, "then I shall have plenty of time and opportunity to reconcile myself with him."

He was happy about this and went to his neighbor's house and set it on fire.

"The knot of hatred must be unraveled in this life!" he cried out. Then he lay down in his bed and died with satisfaction.

However, the Lord of the Heavens sent the golden dragon to Fu-Hi to summon him to the throne. He was very angry and scolded Fu-Hi for his clumsiness. Afterward he had him covered by a large mountain as punishment.

Now you know why Fu-Hi spent a thousand years beneath a mountain. ∎

Once upon a time there were two friends, Hu-Fu and Chen-Hu. They never spoke with another because they were deaf-mutes. The first time they crossed paths was when they were out begging and a rich stranger came walking by them. Hu-Fu stood still and pretended to be blind. Chen-Hu lifted his foot and pretended to be lame. But the stranger didn't give either one of them anything because they didn't block his way. They didn't block his way because neither wanted to ruin the other's chance for some business. After the stranger had passed by them, Hu-Fu opened his eyes, and Chen-Hu lowered his foot. They smiled at each other and nodded sadly with their heads. Then they shook hands and went off begging together. From that day on, they became inseparable friends. However, since they were deaf-mutes, they always held hands, for they lacked the colorful bridge of words to connect them.

However, holding hands was not enough for them, and they both became more and more despondent, for they had never felt the curse of locked-up loneliness as they did now. They looked at each other with longing eyes as if

they stood on opposite sides of a wide river without a ferry to help them across. Indeed, the thoughts of their hearts remained locked-up behind their deafness, and that made them sick with yearning.

One evening, as they walked through the streets hand in hand, they found a bag with fifty gold coins. They quickly picked it up and ran from there full of joy. Then Hu-Fu stopped in front of a candy store. But Chen-Hu shook his head to say no. Then Chen-Hu stopped in front of a shop filled with beautiful silk garments. But Hu-Fu shook his head to say no. Then they both stopped in front of a brothel, but only for two minutes. And so they continued walking slowly with their hearts filled with worry about their wealth. Finally, they came to an opium den. Hu-Fu waved to Chen-Hu and pulled his friend inside. They sat down on the mats and ordered a small silver pipe. Then they looked at each other, trembling with anticipation, like two people about to be engaged. Now their souls yearned to escape the prison of their bodies locked in by deafness, and they yearned to find another in the garden of dreams.

As they began to smoke, they clung to one another with their hands and eyes until the sweet veil of torpor descended upon them, allowing them to arrive and remain with each other at their destination. And when the veil was lifted once again, they floated in the garden of dreams and saw one another.

Words cannot describe the marvels and delights of this garden, because words are superfluous there. The body of the soul reflects everything just as a polished silver disc does. Everything immerses itself entirely into the body of the soul just the way the image disappears in the mirror.

Hu-Fu and Chen-Hu looked at each other, and as they were reflecting each other, they sank so deeply into one another that they were transformed—Hu-Fu became Chen-Hu and Chen-Hu became Hu-Fu. And when they once again reflected one another, the soul of one of them was transformed into the soul of the other. They enjoyed unspeakable happiness.

When they awakened later, they were tired and felt even lonelier than ever before because they had come to know what it felt like to be happily united. This is why they smoked the pipe again the next evening, seeking to depart from the earthly existence that separated them by deafness and to enter into the common garden of dreams. Evening after evening they smoked the pipe. Before long they had spent all fifty gold coins, for opium is expensive.

When they sank into ecstatic intoxication while mirroring one another for the last time, they wanted to remain there and clung tightly to one another. Just as the image of a cloud clings at times to the mirror of the sea and remains there, so the two friends clung to one another. And when they woke up from the dream, Hu-Fu was Chen-Hu, and Chen-Hu was Hu-Fu. They stood up, took each other's hand, went into the street, and began begging.

Neither one noticed the miracle. ■

*M*any years ago there lived a man named Dung-Fu. One day he treaded on some bread and was punished for this. Consequently, after his death he was reborn as a wild beast and lived as a gray wolf in dark forests. As a wolf, Dung-Fu suffered great torment and, therefore, he sought a better incarnation. In his next life he was reborn as a guard dog, and this way he came closer to people. Even though he was only a dog, he could watch the daily lives and activities of people and had more time to think about all this than the people. Then, in his following life, the gods allowed him to come even closer to human existence because of his great yearning. He was reborn as a flea. Now he lived on the people themselves and took part in everything they did. He was even present during their nightly lovemaking.

Because of this, Dung-Fu's yearning grew even more, and one night, as the moon shone brightly into the room, and the scholar on whom he was living had fallen asleep next to his wife, he sprang from the bed onto the window-sill and looked far out into the night. Just then a talking silver fox came by, and the flea greeted him with respect.

The talking silver fox stopped and asked him about his troubles. Dung-Fu told him all about the three incarnations he could recall and wept bitterly out of a yearning to become a human being again.

The silver fox took pity on him and said, "The parents you had in your last human incarnation have been reborn as human beings and are living in the capital city. If you find them and recognize them and are able to bring them together so that they can give birth to a child, you can be reborn as their son."

"I'll try this," cried the flea. "But how can I get to the capital?"

"Jump into my fur, and I'll carry you there."

The flea sprang from the windowsill onto the back of the silver fox, and he traveled with him through the bright moonlit night. By dawn, they reached the capital. The flea thanked the fox nicely and sprang onto a peddler who happened to come by at that moment. The peddler carried him around the city the entire day so that he had an opportunity to see all the people. Toward evening he caught sight of a rich high official and recognized the man who had formerly been his father. Immediately, he jumped onto him. The high official was just on his way to a large festive celebration where he intended to ask for the hand of a refined young lady. There were many beautiful young women gathered together at this celebration. Dung-Fu sat behind the right ear of the official as a flea, and from there he could see everyone and recognized his former mother, who was a poor maiden. However, the high official paid no attention whatsoever to this poor maiden. Instead, he went to the mandarin's daughter, whom he wanted to marry. Just as the high official began to speak of his love in the choicest words, however, Dung-Fu sprang onto the tip of his nose and bit him so hard that the nose immediately began to swell and turn so red that the mandarin's daughter laughed at him and ran off. The high official became terribly furious and wanted by all means to catch and kill the flea. However, Dung-Fu sprang onto the bald head of an elderly man who was standing nearby and from there onto the pink arm of a child and then from one person to another. The high official chased him full of rage. Then the flea sprang onto the poor maiden whom nobody had noticed and who now stood there completely alone.

"Give me the flea!" the high official screamed at the maiden with a rough voice. Indeed, his memory of his former life had disappeared, and he didn't realize that she had once been his wife.

"Oh, honorable sir, how can I give the flea to you?" the alarmed maiden said. "It has crawled under my skirt."

"Then bend down and let me look for it," yelled the high official. "I must catch it! I've sworn that I'll kill it!"

The poor maiden was so afraid and had such respect for the high official that she threw herself obediently to the ground and permitted him to raise the back of her skirt.

Now, the high official didn't find the flea, but when he saw the behind of the maiden that glistened as smoothly as fine yellow jade and was magnificently round, his heart began to beat with such rapture that he could not turn his head away. Moreover, as he kept looking at her, the memory of a former life began to dawn on him from the depth of his rapture. Indeed, such beauty cannot be borne in one short life. So he recognized his former wife in the poor maiden and told her this as he raised her from the ground. Soon they reached an agreement, and the high official married the poor maiden. When they gave birth to a son nine months later, he could already speak at birth, and he told his parents how he had brought them together in the guise of a flea. Well, after they heard all this, they could not be anything but satisfied. ■

*L*aotse means "old child." The ancient yellow man had been given this name because his mother had carried him inside her body in one of his human incarnations for seventy-two years before giving birth to him. Right from the beginning he had white hair, and that's why he was called "old child."

One time Laotse sat on top of the seventh mountain of heaven and began teaching about hidden meanings. All the gods sat around him in a circle on alabaster chairs. They held their writing slates on their knees and pens in their hands as they listened and wrote down his teachings. Golden fire dragons crawled into their ears and crept out of their noses. However, Laotse taught real things about reality and spoke:

"The flower is the reality of the seed,
the world is the reality of the gods,
the child is the reality of the parents.
This is why the son must be older than the father,

for if the son is younger than the father,
the child must begin all over again,
and the lineage will not proceed any further.
The body of the child is young,
But the spirit of humankind is old within him."

Sitting in the circle, the gods wrote down the teaching. Then Laotse continued to speak:

"The flower is the reality of the seed,
the destination is the reality of the path,
the path is dark and the goal is clear.
This is why the flower teaches the seed.
This is why the child teaches the parents.
This is the lesson of the reality."

After Laotse had spoken this way, he turned silent and curled his beard. The gods wrote down everything. They put their heads together and spoke in whispers about the teachings of the "old child," but none of them dared to speak loudly or to stand up from his alabaster chair.

Then Laotse leaned over a little, looked down at the earth, and slowly stretched his arm. All the gods looked down at the place to which Laotse was pointing. He pointed at a powerful Mongolian prince, who had so much gold that he had the courtyards of his castle paved with it. He had a hundred thousand horsemen. If he uttered one word, a hundred cities would be built. If he uttered another word, a hundred cities would be wiped off the face

of the earth. However, he desired to become even more powerful than he was because he thought that happiness resided in power. He wanted to become so powerful that he could command the clouds and the winds and the sun and the moon to do his bidding. He thought that then he would become as happy as the gods.

Laotse pointed silently at this Mongolian prince. Then he descended from heaven without saying a word. All the gods rushed to the edge of the clouds to see what would happen. And so they saw how Laotse was born as the son of this prince.

Even in his crib as son of the Mongolian prince, Laotse had such a powerful glance that nobody dared to approach him. He had to close his eyes when the wet nurse took him to her breast. Therefore, he didn't know what it felt like to look straight into the eyes of a friend. However, his father was immensely pleased and cried out, "My yearning will become reality in my son. His body is younger than mine, but the destiny of my lineage will ripen in him."

When the prince's son turned five years old, he already ruled the will of the people in the land by merely raising his eyebrows. The morning sun and the evening moon came to a stop out of fear and awe when they arose on the horizon and caught sight of the prince's son. And they didn't continue their course until the child waved them on. He stood on a pillow next to his father's throne, and the world obeyed him. Indeed, his father admired his mighty son with happiness and awe.

But then he noticed one time that the face of his mighty child was pale and sad, and he asked, "Why are you sad? After all, you have power over everything."

"I am the loneliest of all the creatures in the world," answered his son, "because nothing withstands my will."

As he was saying this, a bird landed on a branch and began to sing. The mighty child listened, and tears streamed down his pale cheeks. The father was very alarmed by this and asked, "Why are you crying? After all, you have power over everything."

"I can kill this bird and bring it back to life," responded the powerful child, "but I'll never understand its song. This is why I am the loneliest of all the creatures in the world."

When the Mongolian prince heard these words, he rose from his throne and left his golden castle. He threw the crown from his head, took off his royal robe, and went into the mountains dressed in a monk's habit. No longer did he yearn for power. The reality in the child taught him that there was no happiness in power.

The curious gods rushed to the edge of the clouds and looked below because Laotse had not returned. Many of them stood on top of their alabaster chairs in order to get a better view of what was still going to happen.

They watched the Mongolian prince, who had once been so powerful, as he strode into the mountains bareheaded and dressed as a monk. Once there, he found a beggar girl in a mountain cave. He took her for his wife and lived simply and humbly with the beggar girl in the cave. He decided to turn away from all worldly things, for he was seeking the great silence of meaning that is behind all things. This was the way he wanted to attain happiness. Every morning, when he heard the birds singing before the cave, he remembered the words of his mighty son and the tears that had flown down the child's pale cheeks.

But the years went by, and he became old without having attained the silence of meaning. The things from which he had turned away left him, and he became blind. No longer did he see the bird, and he continued to listen for its song in vain. Anyway, he wouldn't have been able to understand what it sang.

And so his heart was wracked by despair. He thought that he had been betrayed and led down a false path. Consequently, he wanted to hang himself.

Then his wife gave birth to a son in the cave. And his son came into the world with his eyes closed already and his hands folded. This is why the world of things didn't touch him, and he only lived in the spiritual world. The child lay on withered foliage and was covered with dry reeds. But the sacred aroma of silence that resides behind all things flowed from his small body so sweetly and strongly that the entire cave was filled with it. When the blind father sensed the aroma of the newborn baby, he rejoiced and sang: "Flower of my seed, destination of my journey, reality of my yearning, you are my child. You have been born beyond my old age. Your childhood approaches me from

the portal on the other side of life. In you, my old age will ripen into the sacred silence of meaning."

Now the blind man, who at one time had been such a powerful Mongolian prince, felt through his son that he was on the right path. When the child was five years old, he went and stood before his father with closed eyes and folded hands. Then the blind father took his wandering staff in his left hand and supported himself with his right hand on the shoulder of the child. And the child led him. He didn't lead him on the path that they had built in the mountains. He led him on the path of his mind. And their steps were not hindered by worldly things. The birds in the blue sky greeted the wanderers as if they were brothers and called Laotse by his name, because they knew him. This was how the child led his father to the bank of the great silence that resides behind all things. The blind man was happy and died.

When all was done, Laotse ascended to heaven again. The gods jumped down from the alabaster chairs, and all of them rushed to him in great commotion with their slates and pens in their hands. And they loudly discussed the teaching of the old child about the reality of things.

Among them was a young god by the name of Yang-Vu. He was extremely ambitious, for he wanted to attain great fame among the people on account of his miraculous deeds. He wished for many churches and much Tibetan incense. Well, Yang-Vu cried out: "Truly, this was an easy miracle to perform, and it does much good in the world. If I see a wicked person, I'll come into the world as his child and become even worse than he is. That will teach him a lesson."

No sooner had he said all this than he descended into the world where he saw a very evil woman. She was a cranky neighbor and a sly thief to boot. Soon she gave birth to a son, and it was Yang-Vu.

"Now I'll show you your reality," Yang-Vu thought, "the flower of your seed and the destination of your journey." And he acted worse than a small wolf so that all the wet nurses ran away without waiting to be paid. He cried the entire day and scratched and bit. He stole and broke everything that fell into his hands. "Haven't you seen your reality yet?" he thought while he watched his mother.

One time he stole money from her that she had just stolen and threw it into the cesspool behind the garden. The wicked woman became so enraged that she beat him furiously and pulled one of his ears so hard and long that she tore it off. Yang-Vu could no longer bear such treatment. So he produced clouds of smoke from beneath his feet and flew screaming all the way to heaven.

All the gods were there to greet him with laughter and scorn. Annoyed, he responded, "I only acted according to the old child's teaching of reality."

Then the voice of Laotse could be heard from the seventh mountain of heaven: "Evil has no reality." ■

Sometimes, at the beginning of the rainy period, there are enormous storms that come from the Gobi Desert. In just a matter of minutes the sky becomes pitch black. Then red lightning splits the sky, and the wind tosses entire villages into the air as if they were dust. Many people and animals perish in the process. When such a storm is at its worst, a horde of wild riders with swinging black sabers can immediately be seen in the sky reflected by the lightning. They roar and charge through the clouds. Then it's best to hide because they mow down towers like blades of grass and tear children from the bellies of their mothers. Red rain falls wherever they gallop. It's their bloody tears, for they're not happy. They are the robbers of divine power.

There once lived a powerful chief of the wild robbers by the name of Dsang-Dau-Ling. He was so powerful and cruel that everyone turned pale merely when his name was mentioned. After he and his riders attacked a village, nothing could be seen of that place the next day other than a still pond of blood with ravens circling over it. Dsang-Dau-Ling tore babies from the bellies of pregnant women and devoured them. It was his favorite meal. He was not afraid of anything, for the magic arrows of his riders hit everything. They even shot down people's prayers for help before they could fly high into the sky as if they were white doves. There were only two powers that Dsang-Dau-Ling couldn't overcome. They were the prayers of the Taoists and death from old age. Whenever some place was protected by a Taoist, the cruel power of the robber chief could do no harm, and as death slowly approached Dsang-Dau-Ling in the gray cloud of old age, he couldn't do anything about it.

One night he gathered together his wild riders and spoke to them: "Nothing can withstand our merciless power. Our magic arrows shoot the prayers out of the sky as if they were white doves. The only person we can't harm is the Taoist, and death is approaching us in the gray cloud of old age. The ferocity of our hearts is powerful, but the strength of our arms is growing weak. We must somehow attain unlimited strength like the ferocity that's in our hearts. On top of Mount Kunlun the god of the dragons is living in the dragon temple, and it holds the serpent scepter of divine power in its hands. If we rob the scepter, we'll be able to attain divine power. Then even the pope of the Taoists will not be able to withstand us, and we won't have to fear death from old age."

When the robbers heard these words, they swung their sabers and screamed: "Let us steal the scepter of divine power!"

So Dsang-Dau-Ling led them to Mount Kunlun, and they stormed the temple of the dragons. There was a terrible battle. The dragons defended themselves with fiery lightning and spewed arrows from their throats like bubbling saliva. Many robbers were killed. But all at once the mighty Dsang-Dau-Ling managed to grab hold of the serpent scepter of divine power. From this moment on, he and his followers were immune against death. One of the robbers had just been pierced by a dragon arrow in the middle of his forehead, and his spirit was about to leave him through his mouth. But it remained stuck between his teeth, and he held onto it tightly. In the meantime, the dragons fled from the devastated temple.

Now, nothing more could withstand the robber Dsang-Dau-Ling, who rode ahead of his horde of robbers and held the serpent scepter of divine power in his right hand. And they mowed down the towers from the earth like blades of grass. They tore babies out of the bellies of their pregnant mothers, and when they attacked a village, nothing could be seen the next day other than a still pond of blood with ravens circling above it. And so they charged from country to country like a storm out of hell. However, their hearts became tired. They became tired from the relentless charging. They became tired from their cruel and dreadful deeds. They became tired from their savage power, for they had human hearts. Dsang-Dau-Ling and his robbers wanted to stop their fighting and robbing and to rest in the peace and quiet of their old age. But the di-

vine power in them drove them relentlessly on and on and didn't allow them time to rest. Eventually, they called their leader and cried out, "Throw away the serpent scepter of the divine power! Our hearts are tired. We want to grow old and die!"

Dsang-Dau-Ling decided to discard the serpent scepter. But it had grown attached to his hand. So he and his robbers had to charge onward from country to country like the wild wind of a storm that never abated, and the divine power in them carried them from the earth high into the clouds. They screamed and cursed like hunted wolves, for their hearts were tired. However, they couldn't die.

Sometimes, at the beginning of the rainy period, there are enormous storms that come from the Gobi Desert. In just a matter of minutes the sky becomes pitch black. Then red lightning splits the sky, and the wind tosses entire villages into the air as if they were dust. Many people and animals perish in the process. When such a storm is at its worst, a horde of wild riders with swinging black sabers can immediately be seen in the sky reflected by the lightning. They roar and charge through the clouds. Then it's best to hide because they mow down towers like blades of grass and tear children from the bellies of their mothers. Red rain falls wherever they gallop. It's their bloody tears, for they're not happy. They are the robbers of divine power. ■

The divine poet sat in his garden surrounded by a bamboo fence and drank tea. It was springtime in the country. The moon water trickled from the jasmine blossoms into the pond, and the nightingale sobbed in its sleep. The heavenly weaver wove fluttering silk. But in many places heaven was so exposed and naked that the shudder of love rippled over the skin of the poet, and he sang:

> "Oh, spring, how much your beauty hurts my eyes,
> For I see you and don't know, however, whether you
>   see me!
> All the days of spring and all the springs of life,
> You are but a long line of maidens who flee me
> And none of you turns her head to gaze back at me.
> New beauty continues to come and whip my heart.
> But none return who already know me.
> I'd like one time to see the same spring again.
> The same spring that was once with me.

For just knowing you is happiness, and that happiness is knowing you.
Oh, spring, how much your beauty hurts my eyes!

At the lantern party there are whirling clouds of maidens.
The silk garments are flapping. A fragrant sleeve
Slaps me in the face. I shut my eyes.
A torrid kiss burns so short that it stings.
Then there is silver laughter far away. I'm alone.
Oh, spring, how much your beauty hurts me,
For knowing you is happiness, and that happiness is knowing you."

When Li-Tai-Pe finished this song, he looked around him and noticed that the night had turned itself around. The rays no longer soared from moon to earth; rather, it was the reverse. They rose from the earth high into the sky and met in the silver crescent. This is also why the trees of his garden were like spears that had fallen from above and remained stuck in the back of the earth. The sweet aromas sank from the sky onto the flowers like clouds of rain.

Li-Tai-Pe looked around and was astounded. The tree under which he was sitting bowed over, and he heard a silver voice sing:

"Oh, poet, the beauty of your songs has hurt us!
For truly, you have sung the truth.

The flying sleeve of springtime closes your eyes.
You only see our colorful gown. But you will never
    get to see us.
Weeping we return into the sky,
Because you don't notice us as we bow right over
    you.
Oh, how much the beauty of your songs hurts us!
One day, when our colorful gown stops dazzling
    you
And you glimpse just one of us sisters,
She will return to you if you call her,
For just knowing you is happiness, and that happi-
    ness is knowing you."

No sooner did the song end than Li-Tai-Pe heard the Saman bird calling from the forest. That was the signal that spring had come to an end. Li-Tai-Pe lowered his head on his arm and wept. He was determined to resist the outer beauty of spring so that his eyes could remain open when the spirit of spring bowed over him.

After a few years he managed to succeed in doing just that. This particular spring, Li-Tai-Pe did not sing a song. The most glorious beauties of April and May were unable to entice a song from him. He sat silently in his garden surrounded by a bamboo fence and drank tea. Li-Tai-Pe kept silent and waited. Consequently, sorrow descended over the entire country as if it were experiencing a drought. But Li-

Tai-Pe waited and kept silent, until one night a spring fairy could no longer bear this, and so she appeared before him. This is when Li-Tai-Pe saw spring, and spring saw him.

Ever since then, to be sure, the spring fairies don't always reappear to Li-Tai-Pe, but he did choose three sisters, and they returned to him in alternate years. Li-Tai-Pe always recognized their colors and smells from the previous years. This is how Li-Tai-Pe found happiness in his life. ■

Once upon a time there lived a customs officer by the name of Hu, who had a middling position as bureaucrat in the civil service. He performed his duties precisely and conscientiously and led a quiet, contented life.

One night, as Hu was in his bed sleeping, he awoke because his straw pillow started to rustle. When he opened his eyes, the moon shone into the room, and he saw that there was another head lying on the pillow right before his face. At first he thought it was his dead wife who had come for a nocturnal visit. He was happy about this and said, "Come, my dear wife. I've been longing for you for quite some time."

Just then, however, the head on his pillow bared its teeth, and in the moonlight Hu saw the bones of a repulsive skull that began to speak:

"I'm not your wife. I'm your father."

"What do you want from me, father?" Hu asked.

"I want you to leave your post and ride to the capital to prove yourself and advance your career. I want you to obtain the highest position in the civil service so that you can wear the yellow riding jacket."

"But I'm satisfied with my position, and I lead a pleasant life."

"That doesn't matter to me!" screamed the skull on his pillow. "Throughout my life I wanted the highest position in the civil service. I wanted to obtain the yellow riding jacket. I did all I could to reach my goal, but I died too soon. You, however, are my son. You carry my blood and have my spirit. It's through you that I want to reach my goal. Get up, Hu! Saddle your donkey, Hu! I want to reach my goal!"

"But I don't want to leave my good position," replied Hu.

In response the skull on his pillow screamed and bit Hu in his ear with his big teeth. Terrified, Hu jumped out of bed to flee from his father's ghost. However, the skull clung to his shoulder, for he had become attached to his neck and shouted into his ear: "Saddle your donkey, Hu! Ride to the capital, Hu! I want to reach my goal!"

So Hu ran to the stable and saddled the donkey. Then he climbed on top of the animal and guided it in the direction of the capital. All at once he heard another voice whispering into his other ear: "Don't ride to the capital, Hu. Ride to the Land of Four Rivers. There you'll find a cave with the treasure of the dragon Dsau-Hu. I want you to fetch this treasure. I wanted to do it, but I died along the way. Through you I want to reach my goal."

When Hu turned to see where this voice was coming from, he saw a second skull sitting on his right shoulder, and he asked fearfully: "Who are you?"

"I'm your grandfather. I want to reach my goal, Hu!"

"But grandfather," the customs officer cried, "my father wants me to ride to the capital. Besides, I don't know the way to the dragon cave."

"Your father was born from my semen, just as you were born from his," the second skull screamed from his right shoulder. "Just as I made the both of you, I can also destroy both of you!" And right after saying this, he bit the customs officer in his right ear and shouted, "Ride to the Land of Four Rivers! Lead your donkey in that direction, Hu! I'm riding on you, and I'll direct you, Hu!"

When the customs officer changed directions and led the donkey from the road that led to the capital, his father's skull awoke. It had fallen asleep on his left shoulder.

"Where are you going?" he screamed into Hu's left ear. "Didn't I tell you that I wanted to get that yellow riding jacket?" And he bit him in the left ear.

However, the grandfather's skull began screaming from the right shoulder: "Hu! Hu! Go to the Land of Four Rivers!" Whereupon his father began screaming from the left: "Hu, Hu! To the capital!"

And the two skulls fell into an argument and began fighting. They kept on biting each other so violently with their rattling jaws that they caused the donkey to rear up from fright and throw the customs officer off its back.

Then it ran away. While the customs officer lay on the ground and the two skulls fought over his head, he heard a third voice from behind.

"Hu! Hu! I want to reach my goal, Hu! I'm your great-grandfather. I married the beautiful Hai-Nu and was stabbed to death on the threshold of the bedroom before I could even enter it. My son had to court her daughter. My grandson, her granddaughter. Now you must court her great-granddaughter. I want to reach my goal through you. Hu! Get up, Hu! Get up, Hu! I'll direct you."

When Hu did not get up immediately, the third skull bit him so hard in the back of his neck that the customs officer jumped up in horror and began to run. But one skull pulled him to the right, and the other, to the left. They all screamed at him and demanded that he reach their goals. They all bit him with their large bare teeth so that Hu, the customs officer, ran around the field in circles until he couldn't move in any direction anymore. Finally, he collapsed, and all the skulls that had now grown attached to his neck just like his very own head began screaming: "Hu, Hu! We want to reach our goal. We gave birth to you, and we'll destroy you if you won't do what we say. Hu, Hu!"

But the customs officer lay on the ground and couldn't move anymore. So the skulls fell upon him, tore his flesh to pieces, and devoured him so that, in the end, nothing at all remained of him. ■

Once upon a time there lived a fisherman in Manchuria, and his name was Sia. One day a fox stole his net from him, and ever since then he fished only with a rod, which didn't help him catch many fish. He became so poor that he had to live in a cave, and this cave was so small that he hit his head on the ceiling whenever he stood up in bed, and when he stretched his arms, they touched the walls. However, Sia didn't want to change his trade, because only if you pursue one course to its very end do you reach the limits of earthly existence.

The fisherman Sia had no light in his cave. This is why the narrow walls disappeared in the night, and the boundless obscurity of darkness spread out around him when he lay there sleepless with open eyes, for hunger prevented him from sleeping.

One night he heard wonderful music. It was as if a hundred soft glass harps were playing. Sia lay with open eyes on his bed and listened. Then it sounded as if a thousand little silver bells were playing. Sia lay there with open eyes and listened. Then it sounded as if ten thousand silver coins were tinkling. All at once Sia stood up and stepped out of his cave. There was a full moon high in the sky illuminating the entire landscape. The wonderful soft tinkling could be heard more clearly, and it came from the pond. So the fisherman Sia fetched his rod and went there. When he peered down into the dark water, he saw that the pond was teeming with thousands of small silver fish. There were so many that they kept bumping into each other, and this was what brought about the wonderful sound of chiming bells.

"If I can just catch five of these silver fish, then I'll no longer be poor!" Sia cried out and cast the line of his rod into the water.

He fished for a long time. The pond was teeming with little silver fish sparkling, tinkling, and chiming in the pond, but none of them took the bait. Sia was very sad. Tears rolled down his pale cheeks and fell into the pond. All at once a little silver fish snatched a tear, and no sooner did it swallow the tear than it twitched and turned as if it had eaten poison, and soon the fish threw itself onto the bank of the pond. Sia bent down to pick up the little silver fish, but it disappeared, and in its place stood a tiny maiden in a glistening white gown. The tiny maiden grew quickly until she became the size of a young woman. She had a beautiful, sparkling white face, and her eyes were sparkling white without any black pupils.

"I've drunk your pain," the white young woman said. Her voice sounded tenderly silver and melancholy. "So now I must follow and obey you, Sia."

"But my cave is narrow and dark," the fisherman replied. "A fox stole my net, and I'm poor."

"I must follow and obey you," was the young woman's only reply, and they went to his cave.

As they entered, the fisherman said, "I don't have a lamp to light the cave, and I have no food to offer you."

Just then the young woman took some scissors, cut a round piece from her white silk gown, and stuck it on the wall. The round piece of silk began to glisten right away as if it were the moon itself, and its light filled the entire space with a silvery mist. As the silvery mist gradually cleared, they stood in a white room whose beams were made of sandalwood, the doors of tortoise shells, the curtains of strings of pearls, and the steps of green nephrite. A large table made of blue jasper stood in the middle of the room and was covered with the finest foods and wines. Meanwhile, the full moon glistened on the wall with a silvery gleam.

The fisherman Sia and the young woman in white sat down at the table. They ate and drank and conversed with one another. They spoke about Taoism and the limits of earthly existence. The young woman taught the fisherman about hidden meanings, and after she already had drunk quite a bit, she also revealed the secret of the pond to him. Long ago the moon fairy's mirror had fallen into this pond and broken into a thousand fragments and splinters. Since the image of the moon fairy had remained in each splinter, all the images continued to live in the water as silver fish and waited for the great gathering of the world.

When they had drunk enough, they lay down on a silken bed and embraced each other in sweet love. The young woman's body was cool and smooth. When the roosters crowed, the young woman stood up, walked to the moon on the wall, and gradually merged with it. She grew smaller and paler. But even when she was already in the crescent of the moon, she was still clearly visible. Then she turned to Sia and waved to him with her hand indicating that she would come again. Then the crescent of the moon became dimmer and dimmer until it finally disappeared altogether. Now Sia's cell returned to its previous condition. However, the round spot on the wall on which the young woman had placed the round piece of silk remained just as cool and smooth as her body had been.

From then on, the days of the fisherman Sia were as poor as ever, but his nights were rich. The white maiden came to him every night. Then one time, when he had grown very old, she came and took him with her on the white path that led into the moon that hung on the wall. And then the fisherman Sia was never seen again. ■

The Moon Fish

Once upon a time, in the old capital of Lo-Yang, there lived two young men who came from good families. Their names were Aduan and Ho-Huan. They happened to have met one spring evening in a peach orchard, and as they walked home together, they fell into deep conversation. When they eventually caught sight of the city, the sun happened to be setting right behind the pagodas, and everything seemed to be made out of red gold. The two young men stood still, and as they looked at the beautiful picture, they were very moved and turned silent. Then they shook hands and vowed to be brothers forever and walked slowly down the incline hand in hand.

When they reached the city, they went to Aduan's home, where they drank tea and wine until the third night watch and spoke about friendship. But they were unable to discuss all the meanings of friendship that night, and consequently, they agreed to meet the next day. But even on the next day they couldn't finish their conversation because, after they had discussed ten meanings of friendship, twenty new ones occurred to them. From then on, Aduan and Ho-Huan met every evening, and they soon realized that knowledge of divine existence could only be reached on the path to friendship, but that this path was much longer than the path of the ordinary human life span.

Then Aduan said to his friend, "Friendship is great, life is small. We must try to attain eternal life so that we can grasp the meaning of our friendship. Otherwise, we shall live and die like that man who had immense treasures in his cellar but could only manage to extract a small amount and bring it into the light of day. As a result, he just eked out a miserable existence during his short life."

"I've already thought about all this," replied Ho-Huan. "We must each choose a profession that allows us time to study and that doesn't keep us from one another. Artisans and merchants must work the entire day. Civil servants can be transferred to different regions. Therefore, we must become street performers. I'll do my acrobatics because I'm very good at that, and you'll sing and collect the money. Then we'll have enough time to search for the secret of eternal life, and we can always be together."

So Aduan and Ho-Huan became street performers, although their families were angry about this and disowned them. But the friends did not let themselves be shaken in their decision. Ho-Huan performed his acrobatic acts at the marketplace. Aduan pretended to be lame, sang beautiful songs, and collected money from the onlookers. They earned enough money in just a few hours to support themselves for that day. Then they returned home, where they sat the entire evening drinking wine, speaking about the meanings of friendship, and searching for the secret of eternal life. They trained themselves in the three hundred and sixty ways of truth. They studied the nine schools of the three religions. They learned how to read holy scriptures, to cast magic spells, to conjure up spirits, and to pose questions to the oracle. They learned to live without nourishment and cleanliness, to balance the forces of life, to rub their navels, and to control their breathing. If they became tired, Aduan would take the lute from the wall and sing. Ho-Huan would lower his head and contemplate his cup in silence.

Years passed this way, and even though the two friends weren't able to discover the secret of eternal life, the meaning of their friendship seemed to them to be even deeper than before.

One night, when Aduan had ended his song and laid his lute on the table, Ho-Huan looked up from his cup and said, "Time is passing, and our lives are becoming shorter. But the path of friendship seems to become longer and longer. A holy Taoist lives on top of the dragon mountain. I want to go there and ask him about the secret of eternal life. A person can visit him only once, and he only answers with a single verse. But I want to try it."

The next morning the two friends said their farewells to each other with heavy hearts, and Ho-Huan began climbing the dragon mountain, which is very steep and dangerous. But Ho-Huan was strong and skillful, and after half a year he had climbed the entire way. During that time Aduan sat at home every evening drinking wine, thought about his friend, and sang sad songs while playing his lute. Then he lowered his head and closed his eyes. This was the condition in which he could always see his friend Ho-Huan. This was how he could know where he was and what he did. Once, when he closed his eyes after singing, he saw that Ho-Huan had just reached the peak of the dragon mountain and was about to appear before the holy Taoist, sitting before his cave and sunning himself. Ho-Huan greeted the holy man with reverence, told him about his friendship with Aduan, and asked him to teach him how eternal life could be attained. The Taoist stared at him a long time in silence. Then he spoke the following verse:

> "The foxhole has two openings—
> Life is its entrance, immortality its exit.
> Friendship whips itself through.
> Knowledge without pain comes only after all the
>   pain."

Aduan sat alone drinking his cup of wine. He propped his elbows on the table and kept his eyes shut. This is how he saw his friend Ho-Huan standing before the Taoist and also heard this verse. He shook his head sadly, for he couldn't understand the verse. Just then there was a knock at the window. When Aduan opened the window, he saw a relative of Ho-Huan, who stood outside and asked, "Is Ho-Huan home?"

"No. He went to the dragon mountain. Why are you asking about him after you disowned him?"

"His family has suffered a great misfortune," the relative responded. "An evil fox's spirit has lodged itself in his father's house and has caused them terrible suffering. One evening, some weeks ago, his father saw something dark sitting on the garden fence. It was a black dog with green sparkling eyes. Ever since then, things have gotten worse around the house. Without warning, a devil's face shows itself at the window, then a blue hand sticks itself through the door, and next the millstone flies into the air and falls to the ground with a loud crash. You can see dog and hen excrement on the food that is still being cooked. The family called two sorcerers, but they couldn't drive out the fox. So the family hung a picture of the pope of the Taoists in the house, and that, too, was of no use. Now Ho-Huan's parents have become sick from the fright, and they are on their deathbeds. The oracle of the god of war was consulted and gave as his answer: 'Ho-Huan will kill the fox.' So now I've come to fetch him so that he can save his parents and reconcile himself with them. But this is typical of street performers and vagabonds: when one needs them, they can't be found."

After Ho-Huan's relative had finished speaking, he left mumbling some curses. Aduan stood at the open window and thought about what the man had said. He knew how much Ho-Huan honored his family even though they had disowned him. He knew that it would cause Ho-Huan bitter pain if he were to miss the opportunity to save his parents and to reconcile himself with them. And so Aduan said, "I'm his friend. I'll take his place." Upon saying this, he closed the window and went to Ho-Huan's father's house, where there was great despair. The parents lay dying, and everything was in great disorder. Aduan sat down at the threshold because he wasn't allowed to enter. He sat there for two days and two nights. On the second night he noticed a tiny animal, smaller than a mouse but in the shape of a fox. As it tried to sneak across the threshold into the house, Aduan grabbed hold of the tiny fox and squeezed it firmly in his fist. However, the fox bit him in such an awful way that he couldn't bear the pain. Since he didn't want to release the fox, his only resort was to stick it quickly into his mouth and to swallow it whole.

From that moment on, Ho-Huan's father's house was freed from the evil spirit. The parents recovered their health, and order was restored. However, Aduan was possessed by the fox's evil spirit. He ran around barking and foaming at the mouth. To help him and to show their gratitude for his sacrifice, Ho-Huan's family consulted the oracle of the god of war once again and were told: "The fox inside him must be beaten to death."

So they grabbed hold of the possessed Aduan and beat him with rods to kill the fox inside him. But Aduan was too fat, and the fox sat inside him protected nicely by the fat. Also, Aduan wouldn't let himself be beaten by strange people. He tore himself away and ran off. So they called his father in the hopes that Aduan would let himself be beaten by his father since he had been accustomed to this as a child. Aduan's father took the bamboo stick in his hand and started beating his son with it. Aduan's eyes rolled. Foam drooled from his mouth. But he let himself be beaten because he had been accustomed to it as a child. However, when the blood streamed from his son's body, the father could no longer bring himself to beat him anymore. He let the bamboo stick fall to the ground and covered his face. The fox's spirit could not be driven from Aduan's body.

After half a year Ho-Huan returned from the dragon mountain. He entered his house and found it empty. The lute lay on the table, and he could not find his friend anywhere. When he asked the people in the street, they told him all that had occurred while he was away. He also heard about the pronouncement by the oracle of the god of war. And so he went looking for his friend Aduan, who sat on top of a dung heap and scratched himself like a dog. When he caught sight of Ho-Huan, he recognized him at once. Bloody tears welled up in his eyes, but he couldn't talk. He could only bark and howl at the sky.

Then Ho-Huan wept and said to his friend, "I swore on that spring evening years ago that I would always be your brother. You took my place and saved my family, and now the evil spirit is inside you. I shall kill the fox, my dear friend, for friendship drives us on. This is what the Taoist told me. And you'll bear it, my dear friend, because 'knowledge without pain comes only after all the pain.'"

When Aduan heard this, he lay down of his own accord. Ho-Huan undressed him, took the hardest bamboo stick in his hand, and began whipping Aduan's naked body. He whipped so hard that the slapping sounds could be heard far away. He whipped so hard that the flesh burst open and blood spurted into the air. Nobody could watch while Aduan lost consciousness. His father rushed over and pleaded with Ho-Huan to stop. But Ho-Huan cried out: "He's my friend. I must save him." And he continued to whip him more wildly until the howls of the fox were clearly heard. Suddenly, a cloud of smoke arose, and then everything was silent. When they bowed over Aduan, he lay there dead.

Aduan's father accused Ho-Huan of murder. Ho-Huan was brought before the court, and the judge said, "Ho-Huan, you've killed your friend."

However, Ho-Huan responded with his head held high, "I killed the fox, but the foxhole has two openings."

Then the judge said, "Ho-Huan, I sentence you to death."

But Ho-Huan answered, "Life is its entrance, immortality its exit."

Then two guards grabbed hold of Ho-Huan and led him to the scaffold. However, when the executioner lifted his blade and was about to cut off his head, a great buzzing could be heard in the air, and Aduan appeared, riding on a sacred Himalayan cow. He lifted Ho-Huan up to him, and both of them flew away on the Himalayan cow, while the people threw themselves down on the ground. The priests rang the bells, played the drums, and read aloud from the holy books.

This was how the two friends found eternal life and became gods. Together they wrote the great book about the meaning of friendship. One sees them often on spring evenings, riding on the sacred Himalayan cow in the clouds. They are holding the book of friendship in their hands. ■

Once upon a time there was a wild and strong robber by the name of Yuan-Dzsau. He was so wild and strong that nobody could withstand him. Courage radiated from his eyes like glowing lances, and they emanated such power that he broke the shields of his enemies with his glance.

One day he attacked a merchant in the forest just as this man was counting his gold coins in the shade of a chestnut tree. Yuan-Dzsau stabbed him to death with his dagger. Then he sat down in the shadow to count the stolen gold. However, the blood of the murdered man soaked the roots of the tree, causing the shadow of the chestnut tree to grow cooler and cooler. Soon it seemed to Yuan-Dzsau as if someone had thrown an ice-cold canvas over him. Surprised, the robber looked up and saw that the chestnut tree's foliage had turned black. The five-pointed black leaves spread themselves like five fingers on black hands that wanted to grab hold of him. Yuan-Dzsau knew at once that the spirit of the dead man had entered into the tree with his blood. He jumped up and ran a few steps away from the tree. Then he turned around and mocked the tree that had turned black out of rage.

"You're stuck there with your roots in the ground," Yuan-Dzsau cried out, "so you can't touch me!"

Then he went home, satisfied with himself, and he lay down to sleep. Yuan-Dzsau began dreaming right away about all the gold that he had robbed, and soon he was shivering with chills that caused him to awake. He felt as if someone had thrown a wet ice-cold canvas over him. The moon illuminated his room. All at once Yuan-Dzsau saw the sharp outline of a black shadow that resembled a large chestnut tree leaf with five points and flashed on the whitewashed wall over his bed. It seemed to have been painted with black ink. For the first time Yuan-Dzsau felt his heart palpitating in horror. He jumped out of the bed and ran out of the house.

Once outside, he made a fist in rage and mocked the chestnut tree again with loud words.

"You can't take back the gold!" yelled Yuan-Dzsau, and he sat down to count it once again in the bright moonlight. No sooner had he begun than his body started shivering from chills, and the black shadow of the chestnut tree appeared on the pile of gold, even though no tree was standing in the vicinity. Yuan-Dzsau jumped up, left the gold lying there, and ran off.

From then on, Yuan-Dzsau led a restless life. He robbed a good deal of precious stones, silver, and silk garments. But he no longer robbed gold. And whenever he

came near a chestnut tree, he avoided it as much as possible. One night he slept next to the wall of a burned-out house and was wakened by chills that caused him to shiver. Once again it was as if someone had thrown a wet ice-cold canvas over him. When he sat up, he saw the large black shadow of the chestnut tree on the moonlit wall. On one of the branches he could see the shadow of a maiden who had been hanged on the tree, and she was swaying in the wind. Yuan-Dzsau jumped up and ran the entire night until the break of dawn, and the first songs of the birds shimmered in the forest air like frozen ice crystals on the water. Just then a maiden came along a path. She was dressed in white and was so fabulously beautiful that Yuan-Dzsau forgot everything and followed her. When the maiden noticed this, she smiled, blushed, and began to run. Her light footsteps stirred no dust; her slender body didn't cast a shadow. After she had gone some distance, she stopped, turned around, and gazed at Yuan-Dzsau. She nodded her head very slightly, and Yuan-Dzsau followed her as she directed her steps to some woods filled with chestnut trees. All at once Yuan-Dzsau stopped. When the maiden noticed this, she changed direction. She went into some woods filled with birch trees close to the village. Yuan-Dzsau wasn't afraid of the people because he had confidence in his invincible strength. There were young birch trees with tender white trunks and small thin leaves that were like strands of a child's curly hair. The maiden stopped beneath a birch tree, the most tender and whitest of all, and she waited for the robber with the smile of a lover's greeting.

Yuan-Dzsau approached her and wanted to embrace her. But the maiden suddenly gave him an angry look and screamed so loudly for help that the farmers in the village could hear her. Yuan-Dzsau, who wasn't afraid of the people, wanted to take her with force. But she threw herself on the ground. So Yuan-Dzsau bent over to pick her up. However, as he grabbed for the maiden, her body turned black and became completely flat and lay on the ground as an intangible shadow. Now Yuan-Dzsau recognized the shadow of the maiden who had been hanged and realized her spirit was obliged to serve the chestnut tree on which she had hanged herself.

Yuan-Dzsau's legs turned so stiff from fright that he couldn't move, and the farmers from the village were already there and surrounded him with drawn knives. However, none of them dared to approach the terrible robber who held his dagger with dragon designs in his hand. As Yuan-Dzsau stood there and swung his dagger wildly, he suddenly had a fit of the chills and began shivering. It was as if someone had thrown a wet ice-cold canvas over him. He looked at the ground and saw that the small points of the shadow of the birch foliage were growing until they became large and split into five parts. Soon they were the shadows of the chestnut tree leaves. Then he looked with astonishment at the young, little white birch tree whose thin leaves were like the curly strands of a child's hair. And he saw how the large five-pointed leaves of the chestnut tree grew out of them like black fingers that wanted to grab hold of him. Now he realized that the chestnut tree had assumed a different shape and had lured him to that spot. Terror gripped his heart. He dropped his dagger with the dragon designs and covered his face. All at once a peasant came up behind him and stabbed Yuan-Dzsau in the back. ■

Yuo-Djung lived in the city of Sianfu and was preparing for the supreme state examination. He studied night after night in solitude by candlelight. This was how he spent the winter, and when spring arrived, fresh aromas drifted through his window. At first they came one at a time— the aroma of melting snow, the aroma of the damp, wilted foliage, and the aroma of the first violets. The smells came in droves. They pushed their way through the window like herds of sheep when driven into a corral in the evening. Yuo-Djung had a very fine sense of smell so the aromas disturbed him. They disturbed him so much while he was working that he sat for hours next to his window and stared out through the black frame into the spring evening.

One night a torrid wind from a storm was blowing. The garden in front of his window was roaring like the sea, and the odors descended over Yuo-Djung's head like rolling waves. He had to shut his eyes. All at once he sensed the entire garden: the aroma of almonds and the aroma of the peach blossoms, the smell of the damp earth and the smell of the birds' nests in the bushes that were cushioned by warm fluffy feathers. Suddenly, Yuo-Djung sensed an unknown, strange, and wonderfully sweet odor under the hundreds of smells whirling all about him. This aroma delighted Yuo-Djung's heart so much that he began tracking it just as one follows the figure of a beautiful maiden with one's eyes as she wanders about in a garden and disappears and then reappears behind a bush. But Yuo-Djung always recognized this aroma among the hundred others just as one immediately recognizes the neighing of one's own horse among a large herd of horses. Yuo-Djung stood up and followed the unknown sweet scent. He went after it with closed eyes because he was afraid to lose the scent. He went into the garden and had to tell the aromas apart from one another with great care and sensitivity, for there were more then ten layers on top of one another mixing together.

Just as one parts the tall reeds with one's hands in order to find a hidden path, so Yuo-Djung had to explore all the spring aromas, spreading them apart along the way, and he followed the strange aroma. Finally, he came to a large oleander bush that stood in the middle of the garden. The source of the aroma lay bunched together beneath this bush. But there was neither flower nor any other kind of fragrant thing at this spot. Then Yuo-Djung bent down, inhaled deeply, swallowed the entire aroma in his chest, and ran back with it to his room. Once he was there, he exhaled and blew the entire aroma slowly into the flame of the candle, and for the first time he opened his eyes. Now he saw how the candle's flame flared up and a beautiful maiden stood in the flame. She looked at him with a furtive smile and sighed: "Alas, you've enchanted me with the flame, for I'm the daughter of a dragon. What do you want from me?"

"I want you for my wife because I love you," responded Yuo-Djung.

"Oh, men are always quick to say that," the maiden whispered. "If you can follow me to my father, the dragon king, and don't lose trace of me, my father will be glad to let you marry me."

"I shall follow you."

"Then you must put out the flame."

Yuo-Djung pinched out the flame with the tips of his fingers, and when they became wet, he realized that the maiden was truly the daughter of a dragon. Once again he closed his eyes and followed the sweet aroma. He walked through the evening garden with closed eyes and didn't bump into a tree because he smelled the dark tree trunks and avoided them. He smelled the cool pebble path. He smelled the resin garden fence and the opening of the gate. Then he smelled the dusty distant aroma of the country road and went forward with closed eyes. This was how he wandered onward. He smelled the fields left and right and the sleeping woods. He sensed the odor of the great water of the river. However, he had to go straight ahead. Yuo-Djung stepped into the water with closed eyes and followed the sweet odor. Then he smelled the seaweed and mud beneath his feet and cool walls of water on both sides. This was how he continued. Soon he felt a bright, glistening light, and he heard a voice say: "Now stop where you are, and open your eyes."

When Yuo-Djung opened his eyes, he stood in the middle of a brightly lit golden chamber. Splendidly dressed princes and high officials were seated on alabaster chairs in a circle. Across from him sat the dragon king on a throne of pearls.

"Yuo-Djung, I know everything. The god of wind carried away Li, my most tender daughter, and blew her into your garden. You enchanted her with the flame and thus set her free. I am grateful to you for this. You were also able to follow her to our palace. However, I can give her to you as your wife only if you're able to tell her apart from some of my other daughters and only if you can find her. Up on top of the earth it's very easy to tell a genuine dragon's daughter from a miserable earthly creature. Now you are to shut your eyes. My hundred daughters will come into the chamber, and your task will be to detect Li's aroma and go to her."

Yuo-Djung agreed and closed his eyes. All at once he sensed the draft coming through the opened doors, and then an aroma streamed into the chamber as if all the silver gardens of the moon had tumbled down to this spot. The aroma was so strong that it lifted Yuo-Djung from the ground and let him sway as if he were riding on waves. But the aroma was also so sweet that he couldn't sense a difference anymore. After a while he opened his eyes again. The chamber was as it had been before.

"Try it with your eyes," the dragon king said, "for I'm grateful to you and see that you're sad. You are to see my hundred daughters and discover little Li."

The dragon king signaled with his hand. Two doors opened, and a hundred naked maidens entered and sat down along one wall of the chamber. Their beauty was reflected a hundredfold on the golden walls. The beauty of these maidens was so dazzling that Yuo-Djung's eyes flickered, and he was unable to detect any kind of difference. Once again the king gave a signal, and once again the maidens disappeared.

Yuo-Djung sighed and said, "Oh, king, the beauty of your daughters makes my eyes tired and blind. The bat recognizes everything in the dark of the night, but everything appears to be the same to a man. And, if a person looks into the sun, he also can't tell the rays apart from one another."

The dragon king responded: "You are to try one last time because I'm grateful to you, and I see how much your heart is hurting. The beauty of my daughters has blinded your eyes. You are to see my daughters in the ugly bodies that they assume when they are approached by giants who like to carry off women."

The dragon king gave a signal, and the maidens entered once again. They sat along a wall completely naked on high chairs, and they were all in the false bodies of disgusting ugliness. They were fat and old, and the wrinkles of their fat were reflected a hundredfold on the golden walls. Yuo-Djung could scarcely bear their sight. However, he looked at all of them, and he wasn't able to recognize the tender ·Li in any of these repulsive figures. Now he thought that everything was lost, and tears poured out of his eyes. The golden light of the chamber broke itself in the water of his tears, and he gazed as though he were looking through shimmering crystal. All at once he noticed how one of the ugly maidens began to change. She became young, slender, and tender. It was Li. She turned her head to the side bashfully because the ugliness that had covered her disappeared. But Yuo-Djung recognized her.

Now she could become his wife, and he also received immense treasures as a dowry. Soon after, Yuo-Djung gave her the name "Tearful Gaze" because he had seen through her ugliness with the help of his tears. From then on, Yuo-Djung remained with her in the realm of the dragons, and he no longer worried about his state examination. ■

There once lived a man by the name of Liu-I in a village near the Bay of Kiau-Tschau. He was already many thousands of years old, but his beard was still black, and he had a glowing gaze. This was because Liu-I had repeated the first year of life, the period in which children learn the art of living, thirty times. Indeed, he had brought this art to great perfection. Every age has its secret meaning, which human beings cannot grasp, because they stay in this age for only a brief time.

Long ago, when Liu-I was born, his mother had a great deal of milk because she was strong and fat. One day, when she approached the cradle, she saw a small, emerald snake at the carved top of the cradle. This snake had a square golden head and ruby eyes. She realized immediately that it was a river god and showed her respect with deep bows. Then she brought a glossy golden bowl with clean sand. The river god crawled inside and said, "I want to drink milk."

So she took the snake to her breast and suckled it. When the emerald snake had drunk its fill, it lifted its small golden head and said to the woman: "I am the river god Tin-Ka, and I shall repay you. I live in the quartz temple on the mountain of dragons and tigers, and your breast is to bear the image of the river Yan-Tschiang."

Immediately after the river god uttered these words, it disappeared, for these gods do not care whether people are happy or unhappy. They come suddenly, and they leave suddenly, just as they please. However, a large blue vein appeared on the woman's breast. It was the image of the Yan-Tschiang river with all its tributaries.

A few months later the child Liu-I grew very sick. The woman became frightened and remembered the river god. So she molded an image of the small boy out of clay and climbed the mountain of dragons and tigers to the peak, where the temple of the river god stood. The blue sky swelled like the canvas of a sail in the wind between gleaming white quartz pillars. Hundreds of clay images of small children already stood around the temple. They had all been placed there by mothers, who had brought them there as sacrificial prayers for their sick children. Even childless mothers came to this temple. They broke off pieces from a clay child, and when they ate them, they became pregnant. Liu-I's mother also set up her clay figure and prayed to the river god. However, he was watching a play with excellent actors at that very moment so he didn't pay much attention to the woman's prayer.

Some days later a childless mother came to the quartz temple on the mountain of dragons and tigers. She looked at all the clay children and remained standing in front of

the image of the small Liu-I. She found it so beautiful that her heart was gripped by passionate yearning.

"I'd like to give birth to this child," she cried and, after offering her sacrifice and saying her prayers, she broke off the genitals of the clay figure and ate them. However, the river god, who was watching another beautiful performance of a play, was not aware of what had happened.

After a few weeks had passed, Liu-I's mother realized that her son had not grown at all and had not put on any weight, even though she had plenty of milk for him. On the contrary, he became smaller and lighter. She continued to breastfeed him day and night, but it didn't help. So she climbed up to the quartz temple on the mountain of dragons and tigers and cried out to the river god Tin-Ka in desperation. All at once he came and wrapped himself around a quartz pillar with his emerald body and gazed at the woman with his ruby eyes. But he didn't recognize her. Then she opened her dress and showed him her breast with the image of the Yan-Tschiang river and sang her song of lament. Now the river god Tin-Ka remembered that she had breastfed him, and he wanted to help her. They both went to the clay figure of the small Liu-I and noticed that his genitals were missing. Then the river god shook his square head and said: "That's bad. A childless woman ate them and has become pregnant with him. Now Liu-I will become larger in her body and will accordingly become smaller in your arms. And when she gives birth to him, Liu-I will disappear from your cradle."

"Isn't there anything I can do?" the woman wept. "I helped you when you were hungry."

"It looks bad," the river god said, "especially since she has just eaten the genitals, and that magic is stronger than my power. But I'll give you some advice. On the day your son is borne from your cradle into the cradle of that woman, come up to my temple and eat a piece of his clay figure. Then the child will grow smaller during the next six months, and after a year you'll have him again. Of course, the other mother will also come and do the same thing. But at least you'll have your son every other year."

This is what Tin-Ka the river god said, and then he disappeared, for these gods don't care whether people are happy or unhappy. They come suddenly, and they leave suddenly, just as they please.

The mother pondered the words of the river god and consoled herself, because if she had her son Liu-I even every other year, she would have more of him than other mothers have from their children, who soon grow up, marry, and go away. Since Liu-I never grew older than one year, he always remained on her lap.

And this is what happened. Liu-I was reborn every other year and repeated his first year of life thirty times. Then the other mother died, and he remained with his first mother and became bigger and knew more about the art of living than all the other people. ∎

*D*uring the T'ang dynasty there was a mighty general by the name of Du-Dsi-Tsun who was known for his sense of justice and kindness. Because he had grown up in camps among soldiers and had spent his entire life in ferocious wars and endured great hardship, he became stronger than all other men, but he had a deep yearning for a woman's warm love and tender care.

One day he heard that the king of the Land of Four Rivers wanted to marry off his daughters and had called all of the noble warriors to his court. The king announced that they were to fight one another in a tournament, and he would give the three princesses as wives to the three victors. Du-Dsi-Tsun decided to leave his camp immediately and take part in the tournament, for the princesses were reputed to be extraordinarily beautiful. And, in addition to their beauty, they were known for being tender and kind. Therefore, Du-Dsi-Tsun saddled his horse and rode to the king's castle.

When Du-Dsi-Tsun arrived, however, the tournament had already ended. The three princesses had just been

fetched from the ladies' chamber where they had been awaiting the outcome behind silk curtains so as not to hear the brutal noise of the combat. Indeed, just as they were about to offer their hands to the three victors, Du-Dsi-Tsun came riding through the gate.

"Wait for me!" he cried out, still in his saddle. "I'm General Du-Dsi-Tsun, and I, too, want to fight for the king's daughters. I grew up among soldiers in the field. My entire life has been spent in ferocious battles, and I've endured great hardship. My heart yearns for a woman's warm love and tender care."

When the king heard these words, he allowed the tournament to be resumed. This time the three princesses did not return to the ladies' chamber but sat down under the jade pillars and watched. They appeared so delicate and beautiful between the slim pillars that the general thought they were like love songs that sleep between the strings of a harp.

"Which one do you want to fight for?" asked the king.

"For the eldest," replied Du-Dsi-Tsun, for he noticed that she was looking at him with ardent love in her eyes.

The combat began, and Du-Dsi-Tsun cut off the arm of his opponent at their first clash. When this warrior fell to the ground and rolled over moaning and crying in the dust, Du-Dsi-Tsun approached the eldest princess to claim her hand. But the princess had stood up and looked at the defeated warrior with tears and pity in her eyes.

"You are to become my wife," the general said to her. "I have seen the glow of love in your eyes."

But the princess lifted her tearful face, and her eyes had lost their glow and had become dim. "Du-Dsi-Tsun," she said, "you are victorious and strong. You don't need warm and loving care. But this poor man, who has become a helpless cripple because of me, what will happen to him if he doesn't have a woman to look after him?"

Du-Dsi-Tsun understood the justice of these words and turned to the king. "I want to fight for the second princess," he said.

At the first clash he cut off the right foot of his opponent and approached the second princess to receive his reward. But she cried aloud out of pity and ran to the wounded man.

"Du-Dsi-Tsun," she sobbed, "you're victorious and strong. But this unfortunate man has lost his foot. What will happen to him if he doesn't have a wife to take care of him?"

Du-Dsi-Tsun understood the justice of these words. He bit his lips and cried, "I want to fight for the third princess."

Now the general's passion flared up so powerfully in his heart that he cut off his opponent's head from the rest of his body at the first clash. Then he approached the third princess, who stood pale as death between the slim pillars of jade. She was silent and lowered her eyes, which were covered by long lashes.

"You are to be my wife," the general announced. "I have won."

After a long silence the young princess replied, "You are victorious and strong, Du-Dsi-Tsun. But the soul of this murdered man cannot wrap itself in widow's weeds of heavy, dark velvet. Instead, it will float about in the nocturnal winds like a plucked feather."

Then she concealed her face and left. So General Du-Dsi-Tsun mounted his horse and rode off into the distance. When he reached the edge of the wilderness, he dismounted and chased his horse away. Then he went alone into wilderness, where he wandered about and lamented with a loud voice. After cursing his strength, he hanged himself on the first tree he saw. ■

I just leafed through a beautiful book printed by the V. & R. Bischoff Publishing House in Munich, a splendid modern work, bound in yellow cloth and embellished with an Oriental inscription whose symbols, read in two rows from top to bottom, result in the title *The Cloak of Dreams*. It is a book of stories and pictures containing sixteen "Chinese Fairy Tales" by Béla Balázs, with twenty aquarelles by Mariette Lydis, a name that had been foreign to my ears until now, while I already knew the name of the Hungarian author through his book *Seven Fairy Tales* printed by the Viennese Rikola Publishing House to which the notable Georg von Lukács, author of that astonishing work, *The Theory of the Novel*, very earnestly drew my attention.

So it seems that we have in front of us *The Cloak of Dreams* as an illustrated book, don't we? Indeed, we do. But thanks to exceptional information, we know the situation is different from the usual state of affairs. They are backwards: the stories are not the ones that are illustrated, the pictures are. They were the artistic givens, and the fairy tales are the improvised inventions that pertain to the images. So the tales are pure occasional writing, prose interpretations of highly capricious designs, and in this capacity they are really remarkable.

Indeed, one must keep in mind that the painter did not assign her literary illustrator an easy task. What baroque dreams, grotesque scenes, ghostly ridiculous, strange and chilling brainstorms! A fisherman in pigtails with a scurrile attitude fishes in a pond at moonlight; a woman squats tousled and striped on a green ground and suckles a baby with her gigantic breast that is interlaced with blue milk arteries; behind the silhouette of a branch of a chestnut tree a murder is committed; scholars with long fingernails ride on a cloven-footed animal through the blue sky; a man stretched out on the ground receives a beating with a stick, his rear is bloody, his punisher looks on with content; a man races forward with a kind of basketwork containing three dead skulls fastened around his neck, and the skulls drive him onward; naked trollops perch like birds on a limb; a wild hunting party of idols and warriors zooms through the air; a squatting man inspects a squatting woman in the strangest way from behind; a very unhealthy page shows opium smokers; another, Siamese twins; etc. All of this is remarkable, original, and uncanny. But a great deal was demanded from someone to make sense out of it.

Balázs has provided a most fitting prose for all this, cultivated and at the same time simple, and the author could really be a good Laotse like the "old child," featured in one of the tales. It's he who teaches:

The body of the child is young,
But the spirit of humankind is old within him.

"The spirit of humankind is old within him"—that is China, and the fairy tales of the Hungarian author are profoundly and lovingly familiar with the spirit of this wise, smart, and childlike humanity. In particular, what I admire, if one will allow me this choice of words, are the poetic dexterity, the successful inventiveness, and the metaphysical profundity with which the fantasies of the painter are expounded and wrapped. Every one of the eccentricities that I listed before—and you can see for yourself—is interpreted narratively in the most ingenious, surprising, and pleasing way. For example, in the story about the man who is driven on by the dead skulls, they are his ancestors that glue themselves to him and want to reach their goal through him and tear him here and there until he collapses from the conflict of their relentless commands and is eaten up by them until nothing of him at all remains. I have chosen this example because of its simplicity. There are others that are better, and I recommend that readers go and find some good time to spend with this beautiful book.

Liu Chang is a rich city. At one time a poor man by the name of Wan Hu-Chen lived there. His parents had left him a fair amount of money, and also his relatives were wealthy people.

But Wan Hu-Chen had no interest in doing an honest day's work. He refused to do business on the boats with dragon sails, and he didn't have any desire to weave silk. He continually occupied himself with scholarly books because he wanted to take the state examination to become a civil servant. But Wan Hu-Chen was dumb. He couldn't even attain the first Chin Degree. So gradually he became impoverished, and consequently, his relatives cast him off. Moreover, they also ridiculed him. This is what we must know about Wan Hu-Chen.

Li-Fan was the daughter of the governor, and her lily-white cheeks had enflamed Wan Hu-Chen's heart so much that he fell in love with her. However, Li-Fan, too, just mocked him. At one point, her father, the governor, intercepted a letter written by Wan Hu-Chen that read:

"Oh, my darling, how far you are from me,
As far from me as my room is from the moon.
Your white image quivers at the bottom of my heart
Just like the moon on the floor of my room."

Upon reading the letter, the governor had the poor, dumb, lazy suitor thrown out of his house.

After this great disgrace, Wan Hu-Chen avoided the company of people and wandered here and there on lonely paths with his eyes lowered. Each night, however, he sat with a sad heart next to a little lamp that cast a weak light on a table with white rice paper and a brown jug of wine. Wan Hu-Chen was writing a book. That's why he had white rice paper and a brown jug of wine in front of him. He wrote down stories about his ancestors and about the famous adventures that people had experienced. They were filled with the ghosts of the dead, foxes, souls of flowers, and various birds. He recorded these stories faithfully and exactly without inventing anything false. However, ever since he had been forbidden to look upon the lily-white cheeks of Li-Fan, he was torn apart by such unbearable agony of longing that he thought up a story about a maiden by the name of Li-Fan, and he kept writing it down with the fine bristles of his brush on white rice paper. To be sure, his Li-Fan was even more beautiful than the one from Liu Chang, and she was not just the daughter of a governor but the daughter of a powerful mandarin, and a hundred maids served her. She lived far away in the valley of the white apple blossoms, and she didn't always laugh. Nor did she like to perform cruel jokes. She sat at her window, pale and full of hope, and looked toward the north where the castle of Prince Wang was situated, as she spoke this verse:

"Oh, my darling, how far you are from me,
As far from me as my room is from the moon.
Your white image quivers at the bottom of my heart
Just like the moon on the floor of my room."

Now it was Li-Fan who spoke these words, and Wan Hu-Chen's heart convulsed with spasms because he felt so sorry for her. "Still, she should feel hurt," he remarked. "She, too, should suffer," he hardened himself.

One evening Wan Hu-Chen's lamp ran out of oil so that he couldn't continue writing. He stuck his brush into a crack on the tabletop next to the wine cup with the wet point of the brush protruding upward so that it would not tarnish his rice paper spread out on the table. Then, with his heart swollen with yearning, he watched the large full moon glide into his dimly lit tiny room, and he watched himself dip his silver finger into the red wine of the cup and stroke the piece of paper where Li-Fan's beautiful name had been painted with the brush. All at once tears gushed out of Wan Hu-Chen's eyes, and he spoke: "Oh, how near you are, my beautiful, sad Li-Fan. You have flown from the sharp fine bristles of my brush, and the valley of the white apple blossoms lies here on my white rice paper.

Nevertheless, how lonely I feel in my dark room. Would you come to me if I asked you? And can you hear me when I cry out Li-Fan! . . . Oh, Li-Fan!!"

No sooner had Wan-Hu Chen cried out than he noticed that the bristles of the brush that stood next to the cup began to curl at their tips and then began to spread out like the branches of a small palm tree. The small water-colored tree began immediately to bud, and tiny black leaves sprouted on glistening black little branches. The moon shone brightly on the black crown of the black painted tree and cast a vacillating shadow onto the table. All at once a small black leaf fell from the highest spot of the small tree and swirled in the cup of wine and then floated on the surface. However, as soon as it became moist, its edges bent upward and formed a small black boat. Soon Wan Hu-Chen perceived a tiny, fine maiden sitting in the boat that sailed toward him over the wine. Wan Hu-Chen placed his small finger on the edge of the cup, and Li-Fan stepped out of the boat onto it.

"Here I am, sir," she said with a fine silvery voice that could barely be heard. "I've come from the valley of the white apple blossoms because you called me."

"Oh, sweet, beautiful Li-Fan," replied Wan Hu-Chen blissfully, "how long, how long have I waited for you here all alone! Look at me! Why do you turn your pale face away from me and gaze continually toward the north?"

"Way up north is the castle of my dearest Prince Wang."

"Oh, turn your gaze toward me, beautiful Li-Fan. After all, I've written you into my book for myself because I love you, and I'm so alone."

Li-Fan extended her arms out toward the north, "Oh, my darling, how far you are from me! As far from me as my room is from the moon."

"Truly, I myself am the one who wrote your words," Wan Hu-Chen said impatiently. "I only invented the prince because I couldn't enter the book myself. Oh, take pity on me. Just one glance!"

"Your white image flickers at the bottom of my heart," little Li-Fan continued to sing.

"You're heartless, Li-Fan. Look, Prince Wang is rich and happy, but I'm poor and forsaken. Nevertheless, you prefer to empty the cup of your joy into that sea rather than allowing me, the thirsty one, to drink from it. Yet, you are both born from my brush, you and your prince."

"It's not my fault," responded Li-Fan sadly. "This is the way you created me with your brush."

All at once Wan Hu-Chen became angry. "Well then, go back into the book. You'll see what happens."

No sooner did he say this than Li-Fan disappeared, and the small black tree folded back into a sharp paintbrush. The next day Wan Hu-Chen wrote a new chapter in his book with the title "The Horrible Death of Prince Wang." In this chapter evil robbers murdered Prince Wang in a gruesome way.

That evening Wan Hu-Chen wanted to call Li-Fan back to him, but his throat felt strangled by sympathy. He wouldn't have been able to look Li-Fan in the eye. No sooner did he lay himself down to sleep than the ghost of Prince Wang appeared to him in a dream and sat down on the edge of his bamboo bed. "You killed me, Wan Hu-Chen," he said sadly. "However, I'm only in pain because of Li-Fan's fate, for she's been left with a widowed heart in the valley of the white apple blossoms. You must help her because her life is unbearable."

The ghost said nothing more than that and disappeared. The next morning Wan Hu-Chen sat down immediately in front of his rice paper, but his brush wouldn't move. What was he to do? Should he write a rival into the book? He spent the day brooding, and in the evening he didn't dare call Li-Fan to him again, for he was ashamed of himself. However, no sooner did he fall asleep than Prince Wang's ghost appeared to him once again and was even sadder than he had been the previous night. "I plead with you, my dear Wan Hu-Chen"—this was the way he spoke—"console the poor, lonely Li-Fan. Even if you've already had me killed, call her to you and love her, for once a woman's heart has been excited by love, a life without a man seems unbearable." This is what he said and disappeared.

All at once Wan Hu-Chen awoke. The moon went through the darkness of his room and leafed through the pages of his rice paper with its silvery fingers. Wan Hu-

Chen got up and sat down at the table. He stuck his brush into the crack next to the bowl and called out Li-Fan's name with an anxious and shameful voice. All at once the bristles of the brush began to curl. The small black tree began to unfold, and its shaking small crown had already cast a round shadow on the tabletop, when the small black leaf fell from the treetop into the cup of wine. The edges turned upward, and the small boat floated on the wine and brought Li-Fan. Wan Hu-Chen placed his small finger on the edge of the cup, and Li-Fan climbed out. Her pale, drained face could be seen through the veil of mourning.

"You called me here," she said. "I've come from the valley of the white apple blossoms where I am now living in the desert without love."

"Oh, forgive me, dear Li-Fan," Wan Hu-Chen stuttered.

Just then, however, Li-Fan climbed from the palm of his hand onto the floor where she began to grow. Soon a marvelously beautiful and slender maiden stood in front of Wan Hu-Chen. Her hair and eyes glistened like black Indian ink, and her young skin sparkled white like fresh rice paper. Wan Hu-Chen was enraptured by her looks.

"Oh, glorious Li-Fan," he said, "can you ever forgive my terrible cruelty?"

However, Li-Fan didn't respond to these words. Instead, she extended her glimmering arms toward Wan Hu-Chen while she hummed:

"Your sweet image flickers at the bottom of my
    heart
Just like the moon on the floor of my room."

"Oh, Li-Fan, if only you could have looked into my
heart," Wan Hu-Chen continued, "you would have understood my actions."

Then Li-Fan smiled, and her beautiful large teeth
flashed in the moonlight.

"This is not the way young men talk," she said, "when
they receive a nocturnal visit from a young woman. If you
want to continue this way, my dear Wan Hu-Chen, then
I shall have to believe your relatives and will be convinced
that you really are dumb."

Now Wan Hu-Chen was very ashamed of himself. He
grasped Li-Fan's clear fingers and pulled her onto his lap.
Blissfully they embraced, blissfully they lay down, and
blissfully they made love until it turned day. As the morning began to create narrow white beams of light through
the cracks of the trembling curtains, Li-Fan took her leave
and returned into the book.

For the rest of the day Wan Hu-Chen sat before his rice
paper with the generous smile of rich people, and he wrote
gifts for Li-Fan into the book. He wrote in expensive embroidered silk garments and finely crafted jewelry whose
thick stones contained stupefying aromas. In the evening
he called Li-Fan to him, and from then on, he called every evening. During the day, however, he heaped gifts on

his lover. He wrote a wonderful lake into the valley of the white apple blossoms as well as a castle made of glimmering jade on the bank of the lake. In the castle Li-Fan was wakened by flutes made of ebony that also played for her when she wanted to slumber, and golden barks carried her over the lake toward the full moon. He wrote love songs for her filled with languishment so that he might awake her longing for him, and he wrote torrid passion into her arteries so that she came to him in the evening trembling with desire for him. Li-Fan threw herself into his arms every night with fiery gratitude. However, sometimes she also warned him out of kindness. "Don't stir up the fire of my blood incessantly, my dear Wan Hu-Chen, otherwise you will be harmed by it, and your youth will burn up."

But Wan Hu-Chen didn't pay any heed to this warning. If they became tired of kissing, then they would sit next to one another on the bamboo bed, and the moon blended the shadows of their feet on the ground. They talked about the valley of the white apple blossoms where everything was so beautiful and peaceful, where storms never erupted, and where autumn or old age did not exist because death had no dominion there. In the valley of the white apple blossoms, the calm of perpetual youth was protected by the walls of eternal letters.

So time passed this way, and after a year they gave birth to a son. When Li-Fan brought their son to him floating across the red wine for the first time, Wan Hu-Chen noticed that the small black bark made of leaves moved deeper in the wine, and he immediately thought that it must be carrying a heavier load than before.

"Oh, Wan Hu-Chen," Li-Fan said as she climbed out of the boat, "I can finally bring you something to thank you for your glorious gifts. Look at our son. But look carefully at what mysterious fate has given back to us."

"It's Prince Wang!" Wan Hu-Chen cried out. "Now I can be completely happy. Your womb has restored peace to my soul."

The hair and eyes of the child were black as Indian ink, and his skin was as white as glistening rice paper. He remained with his father, while his mother came every night, and in this way the years passed in peaceful happiness.

At one point, Prince Wang remembered his former life, but he forgave Wan Hu-Chen. He was an extraordinary, smart boy. By the age of ten he knew all his father's books by heart, and Wan Hu-Chan had to deal with painful jealousy when he realized that his son would pass the state examinations and attain much more in his life than he had ever accomplished. By the way, about this time Wan Hu-Chen was also extremely worried because he noticed that he was getting old. His hair was turning gray, and his face began to show wrinkles. Li-Fan reproached him and said: "You see, I told you that you shouldn't have continued to ignite my passion of love. You burned out your beautiful youth in it."

"That's not what's damaged me, my dear Li-Fan," Wan Hu-Chen shook his head. "We human beings age."

It wasn't the gray hair and the wrinkles that made him feel sorry. Rather, it was because Li-Fan remained the same young age. It seemed to him as though distance was growing between them. A dark boat appeared to be carrying him slowly away from the bank where she stood. But nothing changed in the book. No day passed since it was written, and Li-Fan was just as young as she was the first night.

There was another worry that bothered Wan Hu-Chen. In the course of time his money had completely run out. The walls of his small house were torn; the windows had holes in them. Water leaked inside, and the wind blew through the walls. The aging Wan Hu-Chen squatted with his knees drawn up on the bamboo bed. He was ashamed before Li-Fan, who came to him every night and was clothed in embroidered silk, covered with handcrafted jewelry like a splendid imperial steed. Indeed, nothing had changed in the book. Li-Fan's jade castle did not need to be improved.

Wan Hu-Chen's heart was deeply hurt by all of this. Then one day he discovered that he could no longer give his son, Prince Wang, anything more to eat, and this he couldn't bear. So he took the twelve-year-old boy by the hand and went to the city to place him in the trust of one of his rich relatives. However, he knocked on beautifully carved doors in vain. His relatives mocked him, laughed at his dirty, lumpy clothes, and chased him away. Wan Hu-Chen's heart bled, and he trotted homeward with his son.

As they were walking, they passed the governor's house, and a refined elderly lady in mourning dress was just then climbing out of her sedan chair.

"Whose wonderfully handsome boy is this?" she asked Wan Hu-Chen.

"He's mine. I had killed him in his previous life, and now he's killing me, for I can't give him anything to eat."

"Then give him to me," replied the lady. "He will enjoy a good upbringing in my house."

Wan Hu-Chen wept and took leave of his son, Prince Wang. Then he ambled slowly to his house. There was a cold rain, and he froze and became dirty because of the refuse on the streets. When he reached his house, he turned around on the threshold and looked out into the world.

"Everything is being ruined and destroyed. Shall I also go to my ruin here like my house?"

Then he sat down before his white rice paper and called Li-Fan.

"Why are you crying?" asked the beaming young woman with lily-white cheeks as she stroked his graying hair.

Wan Hu-Chen told her all about his pain and suffering. Li-Fan listened to him, and then she looked at him with a silent gaze in her eyes.

"Don't you want to come with me to the valley of the white apple blossoms?" she asked. "My glimmering jade castle on the bank of the lake awaits you. The sound of the ebony flutes has not abated. The moon hasn't dipped into the lake yet, and not one leaf has fallen from the apple trees since then. No storms erupt there. There is no autumn, no aging, for death has no power there. The calm of perpetual youth is guarded by the walls of eternal letters that cannot be climbed over."

"Oh, but how could I make it there, Li-Fan?"

"Write yourself into the book just as you wrote me and Prince Wang into it."

And that's what happened.

The next day little Prince Wang searched for his father, for he wanted to bring him some strange news. He had learned in the governor's house that Li-Fan, the governor's daughter, had died thirteen years ago just as Wan Hu-Chen had begun to write his book. Later she had appeared to her mother in a dream. At that time she was already pregnant.

"Don't worry about me," she said to her mother. "I'm living happily in the valley of the white apple blossoms."

This is what little Prince Wang wanted to tell his father. However, he couldn't find him anywhere in the entire house. But he noticed that a new chapter had been written in the book with the title "The Arrival of Wan Hu-Chen in the Valley of the White Apple Blossoms."

When he left the house, little Prince Wang took his father's book with him and held it with great honor.

As time went on, he became a powerful mandarin.

■ Bibliography

SELECTED WORKS BY BÉLA BALÁZS

Halálesztétika [Todesästhetik]. Budapest: Deutsch Zsigmond, 1908. See also the German translation, "Todesästhetik." Trans. Anna Bak-Gara and Marina Gschmeidler. *Mitteilungen des Filmarchiv Austria* 2 (2004): 65–85.

Hét mese. Gyoma: Kner, 1918.

Sieben Märchen. Trans. Elsa Stephani. Vienna: Rikola, 1921.

Der Mantel der Träume: Chinesische Novellen. Illustr. Mariette Lydis. Munich: Bischoff, 1922.

Der sichtbare Mensch, oder die Kultur des Films. Vienna: Deutsch-Österreichische Verlag, 1924.

Das richtige Himmelblau: 3 Märchen. Munich: Drei Masken, 1925.

Achtung, Aufnahme! Tragikomödie. Vienna: Universal Edition, 1929.

Hans Urian geht nach Brot: Eine Kindermärchenkomödie von heute. Freiburg im Breisgau: Max Reichard, 1930.

Der Geist des Films. Halle/Saale: Wilhelm Knapp, 1930.

Unmögliche Menschen. Frankfurt am Main: Rütten & Loening, 1930.

Bluebeard's Castle. Trans. Chester Kallman. London: Hawkes & Son, 1939.

Die Jugend eines Träumers: Autobiographischer Roman. Vienna: Globus-Verlag, 1947.

Cinka Panna balladája. Budapest: Dolgozók Kultúrzövetsége— Corvina Könyvkiadó, 1948.

Das goldene Zelt: Kasachische Volksepen und Märchen. Ed. Erich Müller. Berlin: Verlag Kultur und Fortschritt, 1956.

Theory of the Film: Character and Growth of New Art. Trans. Edith Bone. New York: Dover, 1970.

Béla Balázs: Essay, Kritik 1922–1932. Ed. Getraude Kühn, Manfred Lichtenstein, and Eckart Jahnke. Berlin: Staatliches Filmarchiv der DDR, 1973.

Der heilige Räuber und andere Märchen. Ed. Hanno Loewy. Berlin: Arsenal, 2005.

CRITICAL STUDIES

Congdon, Lee. *Exile and Social Thought: Hungarian Intellectuals in Germany and Austria, 1919–1933.* Princeton: Princeton University Press, 1991.

———. *Seeing Red: Hungarian Intellectuals in Exile and the Challenge of Communism.* DeKalb: Northern Illinois University Press, 2001.

D'Alessandro, Marinella. "Il manto delle fiabe: Appunti sulle metamorfosi di un libro." In Béla Balázs, *Il libro delle meraviglie,* ed. and trans. Marinella D'Alessandro, illustr. Mariette Lydis, 101–23. Rome: Edizioni e/o, 1984.

Fehér, Ferenc. "Das Bündnis von Georg Lukács und Béla Balázs bis zur ungarischen Revolution." In *Die Seele und das Leben: Studien zum frühen Lukács,* ed. Agnes Heller et al., 131–76. Frankfurt am Main: Suhrkamp, 1977.

Frank, Tibor. "Béla Balázs: From the Aesthetization of Community to the Communization of the Aesthetic." *Journal of the Interdisciplinary Crossroads* 3.1 (2006): 117–34.

Gluck, Mary. *Georg Lukács and His Generation, 1900–1918*. Cambridge: Harvard University Press, 1985.

Karádi, Éva, and Erzsébet Vezér, eds. *Georg Lukács, Karl Mannheim und der Sonntagskreis*. Trans. Albrecht Friedrich. Frankfurt am Main: Sendler, 1985.

Leafstedt, Carl. *Inside Bluebeard's Castle: Music and Drama in Béla Bartók's Opera*. New York: Oxford University Press, 1999.

Lenkei, Julia. "Béla Balázs and György Lukács: Their Contacts in Youth." In *Hungarian Studies on György Lukács*, ed. László Illés, vol. 1, 66–86. Budapest: Akadémiai Kiadó, 1993.

Levaco, Ronald. Review of Joseph Zsuffa, *Béla Balázs: The Man and the Artist*. *Slavic Review* 49.4 (Winter 1990): 688–90.

Loewy, Hanno. *Béla Balázs—Märchen, Ritual und Film*. Berlin: Vorwerk 8, 2003.

Lukács, Georg. *Balázs Béla és akiknek nem kell*. Gyoma: Kner, 1918.

———. *Tactics and Ethics: Political Essays, 1919–1929*. Ed. Rodney Livingstone. Trans. Michael McColgan. New York: Harper & Row, 1972.

———. "Béla Balázs: sette fiabe." In *Scritti sul Romance*, ed. Michele Cometa, 105-21. Palermo: Aesthetica edizioni, 1982.

Mann, Thomas. "Ein schönes Buch." *Neue Freie Presse* (March 1, 1922).

Marcus, Judith, and Zoltán Tar, eds. *Georg Lukács: Selected Correspondence, 1902–1920*. New York: Columbia University Press, 1986.

McCagg, William O. *Jewish Nobles and Geniuses in Modern Hungary*. New York: Columbia University Press, 1972.

Ralmon, John. "Béla Balázs in German Exile." *Film Quarterly* 30.3 (1977): 12–19.

Tegel, Susan. "Béla Balázs: Fairytales, Film, and The Blue Light." *Historical Journal of Film, Radio, and Television* 24.3 (2004): 497–502.

Ugrin, Aranka, and Kálmán Vargha, eds. *"Nyugat" und sein Kreis, 1908–1944*. Leipzig: Philip Reclam, 1989.

Zsuffa, Joseph. *Béla Balázs: The Man and the Artist*. Berkeley: University of California Press, 1987.

GENERAL WORKS

Greiner, Leo, ed. and trans., and Tsou Ping Shou. *Chinesische Abende: Novellen und Geschichten*. Illustr. Emil Orlik. Berlin: Erich Reiß, 1913.

Kühnel, Paul. *Chinesische Novellen*. Munich: Müller, 1914.

Mair, Victor H., ed. and trans. *Wandering on the Way: Early Taoist Tales and Parables of Chuang Tzu*. New York: Bantam, 1994.

Rudelsberger, Hans, ed. and trans. *Chinesische Novellen*. Leipzig: Inselverlag, 1914.

Towler, Solala. *Tales from the Tao: The Wisdom of the Taoist Masters*. Photographs by John Cleare. London: Duncan Barid, 2007.

Van Over, Raymond, ed. *Taoist Tales*. New York: Signet, 1973.

Waley, Arthur. *The Way and Its Power: A Study of Tao Tê Ching and Its Place in Chinese Thought*. New York: Grove Press, 1958.

Wilhelm, Richard. *Lao-Tse und der Taoismus*. Stuttgart: Fr. Frommanns Verlag, 1948.

MARIETTE LYDIS

Lydis, Mariette. *Orientalisches Traumbuch*. Potsdam: Müller, 1925.

———. *Mariette Lydis: 39 Reproductions en noir et 16 en coleur*. Buenos Aires: Viau, 1945. This book includes an introduction, "Coupe à travers moi-même," by Mariette Lydis.

Montherlant, Henry de. *Mariette Lydis*. Bobigny: Nouvelles Éditions Françaises, 1949.